THE CHRISTMAS KEY

PHILLIPA NEFRI CLARK

The Christmas Key

© 2018 Phillipa Nefri Clark

Cover design: Steam Power Studios

The Christmas Key is set in Australia, and written in Australian English.

ALSO BY PHILLIPA NEFRI CLARK

Christie Ryan Romantic Mysteries series

The Stationmaster's Cottage

Jasmine Sea

The Secrets of Palmerston House

The Christmas Key

Christie Ryan Romantic Mystery Boxed Set

Doctor Grok's Peculiar Shop

Paranormal suspense linked short stories

Colony

Table for Two

Wishing Well

1

AN UNSOLVED PUZZLE

"One moment the wind was a gale, buffeting the cottage with icy air from the Atlantic Ocean with such power I feared the roof might come away. Then, silence. Abrupt, utter silence."

Martha Blake glanced up from the open journal in front of her. Across their dining room table, her husband Thomas' eyes were closed as he listened.

"This was my first winter in Ireland and I had serious doubts about my choice of destination. How I missed summer Christmas at Palmerston House, where the days were long and hot, and the house was filled with people. Here I was alone in a tiny cottage overlooking one of the coldest seas on the planet. When the wind didn't start howling again, I wrapped myself tightly in the blanket I'd been huddling beneath near the fireplace and drew back a curtain."

"What did you see?" Thomas opened his eyes and leaned toward Martha.

"At first, my mind couldn't comprehend what I saw. Instead of the matching, endless grey of sea and sky, I gazed upon an incredible sight. Soft white flakes fell onto the lawn, and as far as I could see. It was snowing. And it was Christmas Day."

"A real white Christmas. How wonderful, my darling."

Martha closed the book and reached for his hand. "Until I was snowed in! If one of the other teachers hadn't decided to drop by and make sure I had some turkey, well I don't know what would have happened."

"Hmm. Snow won't be a problem for you this Christmas." Thomas squeezed Martha's hand before standing. "I might open the rest of the windows and see if our famous sea breeze gets to us before we melt."

"And I shall pour some lemonade." Martha pushed herself onto her feet. "So sweet of Elizabeth to share her family recipe for it."

A few moments later, two iced drinks in hand, Martha wandered through the cottage looking for Thomas. He was in the small entry near the front door, staring at one of the paintings on the wall.

"Are you going to open the door, dear?" Martha offered him a glass, looking past him at the painting. This was one of several he'd painted as a young man. He'd thought them lost forever when his father boarded up the entry and put a cupboard where she now stood. Determined to force Thomas into following his footsteps as station-master, rather than artist, his father told Thomas he'd thrown away his paints, brushes, and paintings. Martha's great-niece, Christie, discovered them hidden in here when she renovated the cottage.

"I painted this one in the height of summer. Remember wondering what a white Christmas would feel like." He opened the front door, then the screen door and held it open. "Care for a walk in the garden?"

"I do." Martha went down the steps to the lawn. "There is something magical about snow at Christmas. After the first time, some of the children would come with their parents to sing carols. And the village was a picture with a big tree all decorated on the green. But it didn't always snow, overlooking the sea. More often it was icy sleet."

Arm in arm, they wandered around the garden, keeping in the shade to avoid the intense glare of the mid afternoon sun. "I'm so proud of your wonderful writing." Thomas leaned down to kiss Martha's cheek. "You really should share the stories with the world."

"I think my time has passed to be an author."

They stopped beneath a gum tree. "You've seen more in one life-time than most would in many. You've scaled a pyramid – illegally, I might point out – and tramped through the wilds of South America. Wondered at the Aurora Borealis and been snowed in with no food on the edge of the Atlantic Ocean."

"I once told you I'd travel the world."

"You told me you'd run away and become a famous writer. You did the former, so think about the latter."

Tears glistened in Martha's eyes as she gazed up at Thomas. "I'm so sorry, Tom."

He pulled her into his arms, both of them almost dropping their glasses of lemonade. "Listen, bride," he spoke near her ear, his voice gruff. "Your sister and my deceased wife are the ones who should be sorry. You and I were pawns and I never want to hear you apologise for leaving again. Understand?"

She nodded, eyes tightly closed to stop the tears falling. "Do you think they were sorry? In the end?"

"Does it matter, Martha?" Thomas released Martha and ran a hand through his hair. "They stole our life away."

"I don't regret my life, and nor do you. It just wasn't what we planned." Martha found a tissue and patted her eyes dry. "I am so grateful for Christie because it was her perseverance—"

"Stubbornness."

"True, and her penchant for solving puzzles, which reunited us."

"And you have your own skills in that regard."

"Well, we still have a puzzle unsolved."

They resumed their walk, going around the side of the cottage toward the orchard at the back. At the wrought iron gate leading to the orchard, Thomas turned to stare up at the attic. "I know you're curious about the trunk. How it got to this cottage from Palmerston House and who hid it up there. But perhaps it's best to leave the past alone."

"Perhaps, dear. But aren't you curious? I'm sure Christie would love to help find out."

The rumble of Christie's Lotus intruded on the quiet. "Right on cue. I hope she brought afternoon tea."

"Do you never stop thinking about food, old man?"

"Not really. Except when I'm thinking about you." Thomas kissed Martha on the lips, holding her against his body until she melted from more than the warm afternoon. He raised his head, eyes ablaze. "I might be old, which is why I need to eat so often. Keep my strength up." He winked.

---

*M*artha led the way inside through the back door, with Christie and Martin Blake close behind. Thomas stayed outside to fill a bowl with fresh water for Randall.

"He couldn't wait to come with us." Christie grinned as the golden retriever supervised Thomas. "He loves the car."

"He'd prefer to be in the front seat," Martin added.

"I don't even know how you fit in it, Martin, let alone with Randall."

"Not to mention the overnight bag and picnic basket, Auntie."

"Did you say picnic?" Thomas escorted Randall inside and closed the door. "Where is it?"

"In the car, Thomas."

"Well, bring it in."

Martin leaned against the kitchen table, reaching for one of Christie's hands. "Nope. It is perfect weather for sailing."

Thomas and Martha glanced at each other. "So, you're taking *Jasmine Sea* for a spin, son?"

"We thought we might sail down the coast a bit and stay the night. As long as you don't mind dog sitting?" Christie smiled as delight filled Thomas' face. "So, it's yes?"

"About time we had him here again. Since you got back from your honeymoon, all you've done is keep my dog from me."

"My dog, Granddad."

"There's the granddad thing again."

"He's welcome to stay the night. Are you going now, or do you have time for some lemonade? We spilt half of ours in the garden." Martha took the jug from the fridge.

"They'll stay for a cold drink," Thomas answered for everyone, and went to the cupboard for more glasses. "We need to talk about Christmas."

They all ended up in the dining room, which was cooler than most of the cottage. Randall dived under the table and lay on his side on the timber floorboards. Perched on a sideboard was an old oak trunk with a rounded top which Christie had discovered in the attic about a year ago. Inside had been unopened letters from Thomas to Martha – sent but never delivered – which contributed to their fifty-year separation.

"So, Christmas?" Christie prompted, although her eyes went straight to the trunk. So did Martha's, and then they glanced at one another with a knowing smile.

"Thought you two might like to come here for Christmas dinner," Thomas said.

"Oh, we'd been going to suggest you join us at the house. Give you a chance to relax for once." Christie set her glass on a coaster. "And invite Angus and Elizabeth."

"We do little but relax, dear." The corners of Martha's eyes creased in amusement. "On the other hand, you've worked tirelessly in your beauty salon since it opened. And I'm sure you'll be busy right up to Christmas Eve?"

"Well, yes. I'm very glad to have Belinda home for her break and helping me, as demand is rather high." Christie's new salon in River's End was gaining clients daily and she had yet to hire anyone else, other than a part-time hairdresser. "The week before Christmas there are group bookings every day for the spa and lots for hair and make-up for parties. But I can still manage—"

"Truth is, Christie, we'd love to do it," Thomas interrupted. "This is our first Christmas married, same as you both, but we've missed so many and it would mean a lot to be the hosts. And there's room for those two love-birds from Palmerston House to join us."

Martin looked at Christie. "What if we have Christmas dinner here, and we can host a party on Christmas Eve? Which I'll take care of, sweetheart. Let you worry about your clients and I'll put something together for our guests."

"Oh dear." Thomas shook his head. "Married for no time and you haven't worked out you don't spring those kind of surprises on your better half. We might need a chat about husbandly things, son."

"A party sounds perfect!" Christie stood and wrapped her arms around Martin, resting her head on his shoulder from behind him. "We have an arrangement, Thomas. Martin cooks and I grow things for the kitchen."

"Good arrangement. You look ready to go and set sail. Just make sure you give us a call once you settle on a mooring spot. Or a text." Thomas pushed his chair back and got to his feet. "Can't have the bride here worrying about you."

They all wandered out, Christie and Martha pausing behind. "When I get back, shall we do some digging about the trunk?"

"Thomas thinks it might be best left in the past."

"But you want to know?"

Martha nodded. "When Dorothy and I were children, the trunk was special to her. I'm surprised she left it at Palmerston House, particularly once our parents moved to Ireland."

"Somewhere between them leaving, and Elizabeth buying the property, this found its way here. To the attic."

"With Tom's letters in it." Her fingers played with the rings on her left hand.

"And those rings. Made for you by George. Do you think he knows more than he's told us so far?"

"Are you two coming along, or does Martin go sailing on his own?" Thomas called from the back door.

"We'll work the mystery out, Auntie." Christie hugged Martha. "Once I'm back, we'll write up a plan of action."

2

TO PROTECT HER REPUTATION

*I*n the front sitting room of Palmerston House, a game of Scrabble was underway. Elizabeth White, the owner of the old bed and breakfast property, was locked in fierce battle with Angus McGregor, Belinda Crossman, and George Campbell. Angus was her biggest issue, not only because they'd played often enough for him to have worked out many of her moves, but because he wasn't playing fair today, kissing her cheek every time she scored better than anyone. Which was most rounds, in spite of his deliberate distraction.

On her next turn, she thought for a while, then placed the letters to make the word 'behave'.

"Well, that won't win you many points, seeing as I can now do this…" Belinda laid out 'buzzard' and sat back with a grin. "I'm going to catch you."

"It wasn't meant to win points."

Angus chuckled. He shuffled his letters, then used Elizabeth's word to make 'never'.

George burst out laughing and Belinda frowned, looking from one to the other. "Are you having a private conversation instead of concentrating on this momentous game?" She folded her arms. Belinda lived in Melbourne where she studied beauty, but was home with her mother, Sylvia, and younger sister, Jess, during the summer break. "Because I came here expecting a serious and professional approach to an afternoon battle of wills."

The familiar growl of the Lotus interrupted the moment.

"I wonder where those two are going." Belinda stood up to peer through the window. "Maybe Warrnambool?"

"Willow Bay, dear," Elizabeth said. "Going sailing overnight."

Belinda swung around. "On *Jasmine Sea*? Well, I guess they must be because it's their yacht, but is it a good idea?"

"Oh, child, come and sit again." George smiled. "She's a sound boat and is well repaired."

"Sound boats don't sink!"

"They will if someone puts a hole in them. I know it was frightening seeing her almost sink, but everyone is fine and the fact is *Jasmine Sea* means a great deal to Christie and Martin. They'll be home tomorrow." Angus patted Belinda's seat and she came back. "Let them enjoy their time together. They've certainly earned it."

The ringing of the phone stopped the game for a few moments, and as Elizabeth went to answer, Belinda decided to refresh everyone's drinks.

"When are you planning on doing it, Angus?" George kept an eye on the doorway and his voice low.

"On?"

"It seems you and Elizabeth have quite a delightful relationship."

"Indeed."

"This town never tires of happy couples." George glanced at Angus. "We love weddings. And I can whip up some rings for you both."

"George."

"Well, you're already living here."

"Oh, but not like… not that way. I wouldn't do anything to disrespect Elizabeth's standing in the community."

"Sorry. One would assume…"

Angus frowned until his forehead furrowed deeply. "Does everyone think that? It didn't occur to me people would, but I imagine it might look as though I'm taking advantage of being Elizabeth's guest."

"Nobody would think so, Angus. You're considered a gentleman, but we don't live in the eighteenth century either."

"I hate to think Elizabeth's good name might be ruined because of how long I've stayed. How would anyone know I'm a paying long-term guest?" Angus tapped his fingers on the table as he spoke. "My intentions are good and I do want to ask her... well, one day, so perhaps I need to find other accommodation."

Eyes back on the door, George shook his head. "I'm quite certain she wouldn't want you to."

"No. I think I must, George. I'll speak to John Jones and see if there's anything suitable for rent in town."

"You should talk to Elizabeth first."

"My mind is made up so not another word on it. I shall move out as soon as possible."

With a sigh, George dropped his head and silence fell between them.

"Drinks are here!" Belinda breezed in with a tray of glasses and a jug of iced lemonade. "Come on, Elizabeth? What are you doing out there?"

"Umm, nothing, dear. Admiring the grandfather clock." Elizabeth came in and sat before her Scrabble tiles. "It really is wonderful having it back here, George, so thank you again."

"Pleasure. It stayed away too long."

Belinda poured drinks and passed them around. "Are you okay, Elizabeth?" she asked. "Did the phone call make you sad?"

Angus shot a look at Elizabeth, who played with the letters.

"It was just Martha." She drew in a breath and raised her eyes to Angus. "Thomas and Martha invited you and me to Christmas dinner at the cottage. With Christie and Martin."

"What did you tell her?"

"I said... I said it sounded wonderful and I'd speak with you."

"It does." Angus reached out and took Elizabeth's hand. She didn't return the pressure when he squeezed it. "So, I'll let her know we'll be there?"

"We'll need to go shopping for something special to take to the cottage."

"George, what are your plans for Christmas?" Elizabeth asked.

"Oh, he's coming over to our house. Mum and Jess invited George, Daphne and John, and you-know-who!" Belinda did a little jig in her seat. "Okay, so it's Barry, and how much fun will it be having such a nice big group." Barry Parks was a local builder who'd worked on the old cottage as well as Christie's salon. He and Sylvia were becoming what Jess called 'an item', much to Barry's amusement and Sylvia's embarrassment.

"I'm looking forward to it, knowing the beautiful food your mother makes every day for the bakery," George said.

"And my unspeakably exceptional chocolate brownies will celebrate the splendid day with the inclusion of cherries, nuts, extra chocolate, and anything else I can come up with," Belinda said. "I might be a beauty specialist extraordinaire-in-training, but creating pastries is what defines me."

Angus and George laughed and Elizabeth smiled, but it was forced. Belinda mouthed 'are you okay?' and she nodded. Her hand was still in Angus' but her eyes dropped back to her letters.

3

THROUGH A DIFFERENT FILTER

"The last time I did this, I almost hit the rocks." Christie turned the wheel slightly and the yacht responding effortlessly beneath her feet. This was the first time they'd taken her out to sea since her return from dry dock.

"No, you didn't." Martin sat to one side, not the least bit interested in what Christie was doing, but intent on her face. "You steered *Jasmine Sea* down the middle of the channel, the way I'd taught you. As you're doing right now."

"I let her drift though. For ages whilst I was below. All the time I was crying and panicking, she might have run aground."

"But she didn't. And you held it together once you focused on the job at hand."

"If you call leaving *Jasmine Sea* where she could be damaged by my ex, then taking Randall with me on a sinking yacht, holding it together? Sure, I did well." Her voice trembled.

Martin was behind her in an instant, arms firmly around her waist. "You saved Randall's life. You somehow kept *Jasmine Sea* afloat with a hole in her hull and a deadly storm bearing down." He tightened his hold. "You kept yourself alive when Derek tried to take you from me.

Start seeing this through a different filter, sweetheart. You were courageous and strong."

She sighed and relaxed against him, as though releasing the fear coiled inside for so long. After a moment, she smiled. "I love you. I'm thirsty though."

"Needy. Bossy. Beautiful." Martin kissed her neck. "I'll find some water."

By the time he returned with bottles of water, *Jasmine Sea* was through the channel. "What would you like me to do?"

"I'm the captain? Cool. Then you are required to prepare the spinnaker. There's a fine wind we're about to take advantage of." Her eyes sparkled and she adjusted her stance to balance as the swell increased. "Afterwards—"

"Afterwards, sweetheart, I'll help you reconsider this captain illusion you have."

In moments, the yacht was in open water and a strong breeze filled her spinnaker. As though desperate to run free, *Jasmine Sea* skimmed across the sea, barely touching the waves in her haste.

"Steady her a bit." Martin called from the bow, where he squatted, hand shading his eyes.

This was like the first day Christie and Martin sailed together. They'd gone the other direction, only as far as Green Bay, but along the way Christie was enchanted by dolphins swimming alongside and fell in love with the yacht Martin had given her.

Along the Shipwreck Coast they sailed for an hour, then another. Close enough to land to see Warrnambool glide by. Martin took over as they crossed paths with fishing boats, Christie tired and ready to hand over.

The landscape changed and Martin searched the shore for a suitable mooring. They came upon a quiet cove, where other yachts bobbed gently and the wind was nothing more than a wisp. Surrounded by old forest, *Jasmine Sea* cast anchor.

"Shall we go ashore?" Martin gazed at the tiny beach.

"You decide. I'm happy here. I'll take some photos and send to Thomas."

"Better make them selfies or he won't believe they're from you."

Christie took her phone out and began snapping pictures. She took a few of Martin, who, in his dark sunglasses, unbuttoned white cotton shirt, and shorts, was as handsome as any movie star she'd worked with over her career as a make-up artist. Even more than some.

"Are you quite done?"

"Never. Ever. You should be a model."

He raised an eyebrow. "Shall I take some of you to send to Thomas?"

She handed over her phone and Martin spent way too long filling the camera with photos of his new wife. "Should be one or two you'll like." He returned the phone with a smile. "Send away, and I'll open some wine."

There were no other people in the cove, only the handful of weekend yachts. Christie settled herself on the comfortable seats at the stern, and gazed at the bushland a hundred or so metres away. The beach was small – like Willow Bay – but here the sand was rich gold, rather than the almost white shore where *Jasmine Sea* usually moored. The gentle rocking of the yacht was soothing and Christie's eyes fluttered closed.

She must have napped for a while, for the sun was heading toward the horizon and the air was cooler when she woke. Martin sat opposite with an open sketch book, drawing her. "How long did I—" She yawned, and Martin turned the book to show her an almost completed sketch.

"Long enough. Now, do you want wine, or will it put you back to sleep?" he teased.

Christie stretched. "Wide awake now. Yes please. And sorry. Didn't mean to spoil our time together."

"I got to watch you sleep." He leaned over to kiss the tip of her nose. "And Thomas sent a reply to say thanks. And confirmed Angus and Elizabeth are coming to Christmas dinner."

"Oh, goodie. Have you got any ideas for presents?"

Martin poured two glasses of their favourite Chardonnay from an ice bucket. "You mean, in addition to the designer scarves you bought for Martha and Elizabeth in Sydney, oh and the designer ties for the gentlemen? Plus the boxes of delicacies I know you ordered from the little chocolate shop we went to?"

"Well, I wanted them to share some of our experiences from Sydney. I loved our honeymoon."

"As did I. Here," he handed Christie a glass. "Let's make a toast to them."

"Cool. Okay, to Martha and Thomas, the second happiest couple in the world!"

Martin lifted his glass. "They might disagree, but I don't. And to Angus and Elizabeth, a couple meant to be together."

"Cheers. Nice one. I wonder when Angus will propose."

"Sweetheart."

"Harmless speculation. Christmas Day would be special."

"What makes you think he's close to doing so?" Martin sipped his wine, smiling at Christie over the rim.

"He loves her. They've both been alone for a long time. She loves him. What else? Oh, as your toast stated, they are meant to be together. So why wouldn't he? Nothing will come between them."

4

SECRET PLANS

A few days after the sailing trip, Christie took advantage of a short break between clients to have lunch with Martha at the bakery. As they waited for Sylvia to bring their meals and coffee, they wasted no time getting to the subject of their mutual interest.

"We're going to need to keep track of what we know, Auntie. I like mind mapping stuff, and am happy to set something up?"

"I think its best you do. And keep it at your house."

"Oh. Is Thomas worrying about it?"

"He hasn't said *not* to see what we can find…"

"Better we don't give him the chance then? Why don't we meet at the salon then if we need to talk? I can't imagine him, or Martin for that matter, dropping in."

Martha beamed. "Clever girl! We'll get to the bottom of this and then tell him." She peered through the window. "Daphne's on her way across. Not a word, yet."

Daphne Jones pushed the door open with a frown, which turned into a wide smile as she saw her friends. "How lovely to see you two out together! Having lunch?"

"Hello, Daphne, yes. In fact, Sylvia is bringing it over as we speak."

Martha squeezed Daphne's hand. "We'd invite you to join us but we're just having a quick catch up."

"Oh, love, I couldn't anyway. John sent me over with a long and slightly strange list of what he wants for lunch. It will probably take ages to make." She sighed. "Better go and order. But you two enjoy your catch up." She made for the counter, stopping to speak to Sylvia on the way.

"We will." Martha glanced at Christie, who stared out the window. "What are you looking at?"

"Angus went into the real estate agents. How odd."

"Your eyesight is good! Anyway, how should we approach this puzzle of ours?"

Sylvia slipped plates and coffees onto their table with a quick, "There you go, ladies."

"Thank you, dear."

"Yes, thanks, Sylvia," Christie added. "Let's see. We need to pool our knowledge. What do we know about the trunk before it was moved? Who had access to it, as well as the shoebox full of secrets?"

"The trunk belonged to Dorothy. For as long as I remember, it stored her dolls in her bedroom at Palmerston House."

"You don't remember it going to Ireland with your parents?" Christie cut into her pie, sniffing in appreciation as steam rose.

Martha shook her head. "My mother took many small items, ones of sentimental value or genuine value, like her silver. All the furniture remained, in fact, Elizabeth bought Palmerston House partly furnished."

"Yet she doesn't recall the trunk being there."

"So it was moved between the time my parents left Australia and Elizabeth moving in. Which is quite a few years, when the house was simply boarded up." Martha nibbled on the end of her sausage roll.

"Auntie?"

Martha stopped nibbling. "The way you said 'Auntie' reminds me of how Martin calls Thomas 'Granddad' when he's going to say something difficult."

"Sorry. I wondered if you'd like... well, I have Gran's diary. And I know I've offered it to you before and you've said no, but perhaps you'll see something in it I've missed. Some clues we need."

It was a moment or two before Martha answered, whilst she drank some coffee, and then dabbed her lips with a napkin. "Sometimes I dream about Dorothy. Almost as though we were children again, but when I wake, it is always to the knowledge she is gone, and we were estranged for most of our lives." Christie reached across the table to take one of Martha's hands as she continued. "I've come to terms with what she did, more than Thomas has about Frances. You know, Frannie was my very best friend. I sometimes go to her grave and ask her why it meant nothing. But then I go home to Tom and understand."

"I'm so sorry. I shouldn't have brought it up."

"No, dear, what I'm trying to say is I'm ready now. I'll read it. See if between us we can discover something useful."

"If you're certain... I'll drop it up later."

"Good." Martha slid her hand out of Christie's to pick up her fork. "Thomas is doing something with the decorations. He decided if we are hosting Christmas dinner that the dining room required more colour."

"A true artist. So, what is he doing to remedy this?"

"I have no idea. He mentioned something about not enough red, so I was most happy to leave him to it. He's missing Randall and needs something to distract him. I need your advice, dear. Elizabeth is my friend, but I am a little bit stuck about her present."

"Spa gift voucher. One can never have enough."

"Except we'd like to get something for them both."

"As a couple? I don't know. They love each other, I have no doubt at all, but they're keeping things quiet."

Martha nodded. "Thomas and I agree. However, we'd like to give them a little... push."

"Oh, Auntie. Don't let Martin hear you say it!"

"Life is too short. And Thomas can handle your husband if he really has to."

"Right. I might need some tips in that department. Martin is anti-gossip, anti-interference. What kind of push?" Christie leaned forward, eyes alight.

"When we were arranging your trip to Sydney for the honeymoon, Thomas collected lots of brochures. He found a weekend away in the Macedon Ranges which might be perfect. Staying at a lovely two bedroom cottage on a lake, it is close to wineries and restaurants."

"Oh, is it near where Charlotte moved?" Charlotte Dean, who helped save Randall's life once and was kidnapped right before Christie and Martin's wedding, recently moved to a small town in the Macedon Ranges to take on a new role in a bookshop. She'd left behind a very sad Trev Sibbritt, the local police officer, unable to accept his growing feelings for her as she dealt with some personal issues.

"Close enough to visit."

"Should I sound out Angus? And you speak to Elizabeth? Or do you take a chance?" Christie said.

"We don't know."

With a glance at her watch, Christie pushed her chair back. "I have to go, sorry. My next client is due in a few minutes. Can we talk a bit more tonight?"

"Of course. I'll get Sylvia to make some take-away coffee for Thomas. And a pie. Because—"

"Lunch is the most important meal of the day."

Christie and Martha burst out laughing.

5

LEAVING THE PAST ALONE

On the bench outside the jewellery shop, George enjoyed the late afternoon sunshine as he watched the people of River's End go about their business. Earlier, Angus had sat with him for a while on his way back from seeing John Jones.

"He says not many rentals come along in River's End, but he's going to speak to the owners of the old place just outside town." Angus had pointed in the direction toward the mountains. "Been on the market for a couple of years, so they might as well make some income."

"Isn't that where Bernie Cooper holed up for weeks on end?" George remembered all too well the young man who'd disrupted Christie and Martin's wedding, not to mention threatened half the town, including himself. "It's a bit secluded."

"Which is why having someone living there might be good. And it will only be until Elizabeth and I are ready for... well, for a proper commitment."

"So, she's alright with this arrangement, Angus?"

From the way his friend's expression changed, he'd known the answer. "You've not told her. I've never married, so ignore my advice if you wish, but it seems risky to withhold such important information from her."

Angus nodded. "Good advice, George. Why did you never marry?"

The question still had him pondering a few hours later. He'd told Angus he'd never met the right woman, but had left out a few words. He'd never met the right woman who returned his feelings. And once Frances Williams set her sights on Thomas, he wasn't about to interfere. The sad thing was, while Thomas yearned for his lost love with Martha, George saw Frannie with him every day and wondered where all their lives would be had the fateful night on the beach in 1967 not occurred.

"George? You okay?" Christie dropped onto the bench beside him, shaking him from his thoughts.

"Are you closed already?"

"Belinda threw me out." She laughed. "She had the last client of the day and insisted she'd clean up and close."

"So you're on your way home to my godson."

"Soon. I am so glad to catch you."

"How may I help?" Christie was one of his favourite people, one whose resilience and determination was matched only by the kindness in her heart. "Is it a new puzzle?"

"An old one, actually." She rummaged in her bag for sunglasses.

His smile faded. These days his mind wandered to the past often and not always to good memories. "I'm listening."

"I've been meaning to ask you for so long, but now Martha and I are hoping to get to the bottom of how the trunk got into the attic of the cottage."

George sucked his breath in.

Why now?

Some things should be left untold.

"We know the trunk belonged to Dorothy and speculate it was left behind in Palmerston House when she moved to Melbourne, and her parents left for Ireland." Christie waved to Daphne, watering her pot plants lining the outside of the real estate agency. "Gran had the letters from Thomas to Martha."

"Are you certain?"

"Yes. She admitted as much in the diary she left me. But Frannie had the rings."

"No. I'm certain she sold them."

Christie tilted her head. "Do you recall the first time we met, George? I came here looking for information on those rings and you said you thought 'she'd sold them'. I thought you meant Martha."

"I meant Frances. This isn't a comfortable subject."

"I'm sorry. I wouldn't ask, but Martha really wants to know. And so does Thomas, except he's concerned about upsetting Martha."

"Wouldn't want to hurt either of them." He sighed heavily. "It was close to Christmas and Thomas junior was only a few months old."

---

1 *970*

George finished wrapping a small jewellery box in ornate Christmas paper, then handed it to his customer with a smile. "You will be a very popular man on Christmas Day, sir."

Once his customer left, he realised Frances was in the shop, admiring a row of elegant diamond rings. She looked up with a smile as he approached. "These are so beautiful, George. I mean, I do love the ring Thomas chose, but these ones are very special."

"Are you looking for a present today?"

Frannie frowned and glanced over her shoulder at the door. "Actually, I'm selling."

"Selling?" George's heart sank as she pulled a familiar pouch from her bag. "Oh, don't open it, please, Frances."

But open it she did, sliding out the ring box he'd once given Thomas. He struggled to look away, still proud of the engagement and wedding rings he'd crafted for Thomas, his closest friend.

"Why do you have them?"

"Thomas won't get rid of them. I asked him once and he didn't speak to me for a whole day. But they are in the bottom drawer and will never see the

light of day. What are they worth, George? I could use some extra money now Thomas junior is here."

George turned away, appalled. *"Those don't belong to you, so please return them to Thomas."*

"I just told you—"

"They were a gift for him and Martha. I won't discuss this any further." He went around the counter and stared at her, disappointment mingling with anger. *"Did you ever find it, Frances?"*

"Find what?" She returned the rings to the pouch, then her bag.

"The pendant I made you."

"Oh, how long ago was that, George?" Frannie laughed. *"I do remember it, the cute little F you designed. Well, I thought you might want these, but no doubt there's another jeweller who will buy them."*

"Please don't."

"Martha is gone, George. I'm the woman Thomas chose and it's time everyone accepts it."

How could he ever forget? But why Thomas chose Frannie was a mystery until Christie came to town and discovered the truth that Frannie and Dorothy Ryan conspired to make it happen. Yet part of him always loved Frannie and the day she died, he mourned her. And afterwards.

"George?" Christie asked. "Any thoughts?"

"Frannie offered me the rings to buy. I said no, of course, and left her in no doubt they belonged to Thomas. But she had a new baby and Thomas was an unknown artist, so money was tight. Always thought she'd found a buyer until…"

"Until I appeared with them."

He nodded. "I was so pleased to see them and now they are back on Martha's finger, where they belong."

"So, now I need to work out whether Frannie ended up with the letters, or Gran kept them, but got the rings as well."

6

ANGUS AND ELIZABETH

"I feel sometimes this is a perpetual exercise, putting up decorations and then packing them away." Elizabeth was in the middle of the foyer, boxes of Christmas decorations around her feet. "First for Christie and Martin's engagement party that didn't happen, then the one that did, and then for their wedding—"

"Which was divine." Angus mentioned from his perch up a stepladder near the Christmas tree.

"As weddings must be. And now Christmas."

"And you had Thomas and Martha's wedding at the beginning of the year."

"Perhaps I should leave them up all the time."

"There is nothing as pretty as the beautiful traditional colours you've chosen." Angus climbed down to collect an armful of tinsel. "Red, green, and gold. Perfect."

"You stay up there and I'll pass to you." Elizabeth picked up a box. "I'm so glad the last of the guests will be heading off before Christmas Day though. I love it so much, but it should be shared with family and friends."

"Indeed. There were many years I prepared Miss Dorothy's house and cared for her guests, but not once did she look happy or offer a word of Christmas cheer to me. Christie was her only family and not even allowed to sit at the table with the adults until the last couple of years, so she joined me in the kitchen and in between serving courses, we'd have our own celebration."

Elizabeth dropped the tinsel she was holding and burst into tears.

Angus almost fell off the stepladder in his haste to reach the ground and put his arms around her. "Dear lady, I didn't mean to upset you!"

For a few moments, she sobbed against his chest, then pulled away to blow her nose. "How far does the wickedness of Dorothy Ryan go? Will there be no end to stories of her behaviour?"

"I didn't know you felt this way, Elizabeth, or I'd have said nothing. Please, here, have another handkerchief."

"Thanks." She dabbed her eyes, taking deep breaths to calm herself. "After what she did to poor Martha and Thomas, then turning her back on her own daughter, and raising Christie without warmth and love... oh, and how she must have treated you, Angus."

"She paid me well, left me to run the house and care for Christie, and mellowed in her last years. I've worked for worse employers and besides, Christie and I are fine." He glanced at the grandfather clock. "Is it too early for a sherry?"

"Never."

"I'll arrange it whilst you freshen up." He kissed her cheek. "Be right back."

Elizabeth watched him until he was out of sight, then touched her cheek and whispered, "Please don't leave."

A little later and after several sips of sherry, Elizabeth stood back from the tree. "I think it is done, don't you?"

"Shall we try it with the lights on?"

Angus flicked the switch and joined Elizabeth. The tree was over twelve feet tall and nestled in the curve of the sweeping staircase. A myriad of coloured lights pulsed amongst the branches, bringing to life the beautiful ornaments thickly adorning the tree. Both smiled in response, their eyes travelling over the tree, and then to each other. "I should hang some mistletoe," Angus teased.

Tears glistened again in Elizabeth's eyes. "Do you need a reason?"

With a hand on either side of her face, Angus kissed Elizabeth's lips until she forgot she was in the centre of the foyer. When he drew back a fraction to stare into her eyes, his own were serious. "Why so sensitive today? I'm not used to tears from you."

"Umm… Christmas. Always makes me emotional."

"Then I shall be your strength. No more decorating tonight. Let's go out for dinner."

"To the pub?"

"Wherever you choose."

"Then I choose the pub."

"Shall we walk? That way we can select a nice bottle of wine and not worry about a car."

Elizabeth nodded. "I'll put the boxes away—"

"No, I'll take care of it."

"Oh, then I might have a quick shower. Are you sure?"

"Quite certain." Angus began packing the boxes up. "Then we can talk about Christmas over dinner."

---

*L*ance, who owned the local hotel, was a wonderful host. As soon as Elizabeth and Angus arrived, he escorted them to their favourite table, the quietest in the otherwise noisy bistro. Seated opposite sides of the small table near the window, Angus selected the wine at Elizabeth's request, knowing how well he always chose. Dinner ordered, they held hands across the table.

"Shall we discuss Christmas?"

"It's only just over a week away, so yes." Elizabeth smiled. "How sweet of Thomas and Martha to include us at the cottage."

"And there's Christmas Eve at Christie and Martin's. He said something about a buffet."

"I think it would be nice to help Martin. I know he's a fabulous cook, but there'll be a lot of people there. And I'm not committed to anything at Palmerston House."

"Good idea. Shall we see if he's free tomorrow and we can make some plans?"

"If you are." Elizabeth picked up her wine glass.

Angus' forehead wrinkled. "Well, yes. Is something worrying you?"

Only hearing you say you were moving out.

"You've done so much to help me, Angus. Been there time and again. Making breakfasts for the guests with me, helping decorate, putting yourself out when you are paying to live at Palmerston House."

Dinner arrived. Lance placed their respective plates with a flourish and a 'Bon appetite' before topping up their glasses. All the time, Elizabeth felt Angus' eyes on her. As soon as they were alone, she spoke again. Too quickly. "Of course, I love the help. I love having you here. I mean, there. At Palmerston House."

He smiled. "You must keep in mind I am by nature, a helper. A lifetime in service and still, I do enjoy it." The smile dropped. "Have I overstepped?"

"Angus, no!" Elizabeth noticed another diner turn their head. "Sorry, I didn't mean to be so loud. It wasn't what I meant at all. I don't know how to say what I want to."

Calm down and talk to him. You love him, Elizabeth.

Instead, she concentrated on swirling pasta onto her fork.

"Elizabeth White, there is nothing you can say to upset or offend me. Not a thing. So, speak freely." Angus hadn't started his meal, not even picked up a fork, but the hand holding his wine glass shook ever so slightly.

Elizabeth took a deep breath. "I'd rather you don't pay me anymore. In fact, I won't accept any further payment. Palmerston House is your home for as long as you wish to stay."

There, it was said.

"And before you say anything, please think about it. Let's have our lovely dinner and then we can talk further. When you wish."

Angus picked up his fork, his eyes never leaving Elizabeth's. "I agree. We should enjoy this dinner and perhaps, over a cup of tea in the morning, discuss this further."

7

DOROTHY'S DIARY

*T*homas proudly displayed his efforts in the dining and lounge rooms to Christie. The mouth-watering aroma of Martha's famous chili wafted through the cottage and Christie's stomach rumbled.

"I heard that. Doesn't my grandson feed you?" Thomas flicked on the light in the lounge room.

"He's cooking right now. We went for a walk with Randall once I got home and then remembered I needed to run over here."

"To see my handiwork?"

"It looks amazing, Thomas!"

Dominating the comfortable if small lounge room was a dark green tree, decorated with red and gold bows, ornaments, and tinsel. Old-fashioned and traditional. A row of stockings hung from the marble mantelpiece, and Christmas cards sat upon it.

"And this is where we will enjoy Christmas dinner, and it can't come too soon."

In the dining room, the theme continued with thick red tinsel scalloped against the walls, held up by bows. Gold star ornaments dangled from the ceiling. "We have some lovely linen to dress the table, and will bring some of the waratah in for a real Australian feel."

"You've made the cottage look so festive. I noticed the wreath on the front door, and love the little touches everywhere."

"Thanks," Thomas looked pleased with himself. "Before it gets completely dark, I might finish putting lights on the back porch."

They wandered to the kitchen, where Martha stirred the chili. "Half an hour, dear."

"I'll be here." Thomas grinned and went through the back door.

"Did you think about how to approach Angus and Elizabeth, Auntie?" Christie leaned against a chair, watching Martha and longing for a taste of chili.

As if she knew, Martha scooped some into a small bowl and handed it to Christie. "Not done, not hot enough yet, but you look starving."

"Thanks, I am. And I'll go in a minute." Christie took a mouthful and closed her eyes in bliss. "So... good."

"Thomas thinks we should give them the holiday. Let them work it out."

"What do you think?"

"Elizabeth never takes a break, so I'll support Tom's thinking. If they don't wish to use it together, I'm sure they can compromise." Martha turned the heat down and put a lid onto the pot. "You brought the diary?"

Christie put the bowl on the table and opened her handbag. "I just hope it isn't too... well, upsetting. She writes about you a lot."

Martha expression revealed nothing. "I'm mostly interested in any comments about the trunk, or at least the shoebox everything was kept in." She glanced at the back door as Christie held the diary out. "He doesn't know. I will show it to him, but not yet."

"I won't say anything." It hurt Christie to see Martha's hands shake as she took the small book and stared at it.

What are you feeling?

Estranged from Gran for some fifty years, how odd it must be to hold her sister's diary from 1968.

"Thank you, dear. I'm going to put in somewhere safe if you'll watch the chili for a moment."

"Of course." Christie gave Martha a quick hug, then turned to the stove. "If I don't eat it all by myself!"

———

*M*uch later, once Thomas went to bed complaining about Martha's night-owl habits, she took the diary to the lounge room and sat on the chair closest to the tree. Under lamp light, Martha opened her late sister's private diary. January 1968 – only weeks after Martha had run away from Thomas and their engagement on River's End beach in the middle of a storm.

The purpose of reading this was to find even one small clue she and Christie could follow to discover how the trunk and its contents got to this very cottage she now sat in. Nobody lived here for many years, nobody even came to tend the gardens, so when Dorothy left it to Christie, the property was in a dreadful state of disrepair.

Martha's heartbeat was heavy in her chest as she opened to the first entry.

1st January 1968. Martha is still here with me. Still fussing about Thomas and what happened that night and fretting he has not been in touch. If I had given her even one of the letters he has written, no doubt she would have gone running back to River's End. Every time one arrives, I remind myself this is for her own benefit. In spite of his actions that saved her life, the man is not suited to Martha, and one day she will understand. She cried at Christmas time but is otherwise beginning to cheer up and even came out with me last night to celebrate the New Year.

"Cheer up? Oh, Dorothy!" Martha closed the diary with some force. The New Year celebration was under duress, with Dorothy insisting she come out. There was no joy in the occasion, only a numbness she remembered to this day. Perhaps reading this was a mistake. Yet, Martha now needed to know. To understand. One by one, she read the entries about herself.

21st January 1968. I almost gave in. Yesterday, Martha and Thomas should have been married. She would not get out of bed until last night and sat by the window with tears going down her face for hours. Why she has not got on a train and gone back to talk to the boy is beyond me. Pride and probably fear of rejection I suppose. It made me think about what I have done to her.

20th February 1968. I am getting frustrated with Martha. In spite of my encouragement for her to find a job or study she likes, her heart stays with Thomas Blake. There must be a way to break this bond and free Martha to find a new future. Frances has insisted on meeting with me this week, and although I cannot stand the girl, she helped before and might help again.

26th February 1968. Frances has a suggestion I struggle to agree to. Keeping letters from my sister is one thing, but to be party to an outright lie? It is clear Frances has strong feelings herself for Thomas Blake, but she refused to reply when I asked if he returns them. I suspect he does not.

28th March 1968. It is done. Martha never wants to see Thomas again, and I stood by and let that happen. I thought I would be happy this day has finally come, but the light has gone out of my sister's eyes. The hope, the love and her irrepressible joy of living have been extinguished. I cannot repair this, and I can never, ever let her know the truth. All I hope is one day she understands I do love her so much.

Love? Martha set the diary on the side of the armchair and pushed herself to her feet. There was no love in Dorothy. Only a selfish desire to control the life of her younger sister and keep their mother happy. She helped herself to a glass of brandy from their small bar, then sat again. If only she'd known, even had an inkling of what was going on in the background. Too naive and proud.

Too stubborn and hot-headed.

And the result was a lifetime without Tom.

8

RELUCTANT HELPER

*M*artin surfed whilst Randall ran up and down the tideline, chasing seagulls, paddling, and occasionally barking for the sheer joy of it. The day would warm quickly once the sun was further above the horizon, but for the moment, the air was comfortable.

Thomas strolled along the wet sand, sandals in one hand and water bottle in the other. Randall raced in his direction. By the time Martin caught his final wave in, they were sitting on higher ground, where he'd left his towel and bag, deep in conversation.

"What are you two plotting?" Panting slightly, Martin carried his board to where they sat.

Thomas offered Martin his water bottle. "Have mine, I gave the dog the rest of yours."

"There's more in the other pocket. But thanks."

"Seeing as the dog here doesn't have a collar, he must be a stray. Think he'd like to come home with me."

Martin shook his head, lips curving. He found his own water and took a long drink, reaching out to pat Randall when he put it back. "Does he look like a stray?"

"Looks like he needs a good feed."

"If he lived with you, he'd be the size of a house. He's fit, Thomas. Feel those muscles."

"Ah," Thomas patted his own stomach. "Like mine."

Randall spotted a stick and tore off to retrieve it.

"Have you considered getting a dog? It is years since you had one." Martin towelled his hair.

"You could just give Randall to me. Okay. I know. All joking aside, I'm not sure how Martha would feel. She loves him, of course, but a puppy might be asking too much. Might need to keep sharing him."

"Well, you are most welcome to do so. What are you doing down here so early, Thomas?"

Thomas picked up a handful of sand and let it trickle through his fingers. "The bride was up late, reading a book. Still asleep when I got up, so thought I'd have a walk. I'm thinking."

"About?"

"The distant past. And how the trunk got into the attic."

"Does everyone need to solve puzzles?" Martin took a T-shirt from the bag and slipped it over his head. "Does it matter now? You have the letters and rings back."

"It's not about having them back. I need this to be... over."

They sat for a while in silence, until Randall returned and flopped between them. Both men automatically patted him and he grunted in pleasure.

"You said you need this to be over," Martin said. "Is resolving these last unanswered questions going to ease your mind, let you forgive, at last?"

With a heavy sigh, Thomas nodded, his eyes on the ocean. "Doesn't matter how happy I am now, son. I need to understand. Find the key to what happened. I know Martha is curious but I'd like to protect her from being hurt any more. If I know, then I can break it to her more gently."

"I'll help you."

Thomas turned to Martin in surprise. "You will?"

"Don't tell Christie. At least, not yet. I spend enough time suggesting she worry less about others and don't need it turned around on me."

With a short laugh, Thomas got to his feet and stretched. "Our secret, son."

"I'll walk with you." Randall rolled around on the sand, but leapt up and followed once they headed off. "Where do we start looking?"

"I'd like to take another look at the shoebox the rings and letters were kept in all those years."

"What's special about it?"

"Might spark off a memory."

"Don't you have it?"

"Christie has it."

"She does?"

"Asked her to keep the letters. Eventually Martha and I will want them, but there's some... emotional stuff in them. Never felt right having them in the cottage for some reason."

"Ask her for them."

"Only want to look at the shoebox, son."

"I can have a look around and see if I can find it, then you come over and look to your hearts content."

"Thanks. I'm going to talk to George later on today. Around whiskey time."

"Not sure what he'd know."

Thomas stopped and waited for Randall to return the stick, then he threw it. "Your godfather had a soft spot for your grandmother. Reckon if things had been different, he might have pursued her himself."

"And this is why I stay out of other people's business."

"Sorry, son. Don't mean to upset your view of the world. But George is a gentleman and my best friend. He'd never step over that line."

"Well, you have your chat with him and I'll look for the shoebox." Martin stopped. "I might get the boy home, it's warming up."

"Remember to collect your surfboard. What would you like for Christmas?"

Martin hugged Thomas. "All of my family happy and healthy. Doesn't get any better than this."

9

FIRST CLUE

*O*ut in the garden in the cool of early morning, Martha turned the soil in a new vegetable bed with a shovel. She forced it into the soft ground, then flicked it over and repeated. She'd woken to an empty house, exhausted when she finally fell into bed well after two. Thomas left a note so she imagined he'd be home in the next half hour and ready for breakfast. Until then, she needed to dig.

At the end of Dorothy's diary was a letter. One Dorothy penned to Martha to explain herself. Unable to bear reading it properly, she'd skimmed over the pages as she drank two glasses of brandy, eventually finding one paragraph important enough to reread. It was about Frannie.

After her son was born, she begged me for the letters, wanting to keep them with Martha's wedding and engagement rings. She was guilt-ridden and terrified you would find out what we did. She told me how she fooled Thomas into giving up on you...

"Guilt-ridden my foot." Martha sliced a large clod of soil in half. Without doubt Frannie was frightened of being caught out. There'd been no risk at all in leaving the letters with Dorothy, as once Martha left Australia, she didn't return. Not until Dorothy died.

But who would know I'd stay away so long?

Frannie's fear must have clouded common sense. If she'd had any.

Why would Frannie believe the letters were safer with her? If Thomas found them, she'd risk him turning his back on his wife and child and seeking out his first love, regardless of her being on the other side of the world.

This was a clue. Martha stopped digging, almost out of breath. Why had Frannie believed the letters would be in a better place with her than with Dorothy? Both women had secrets to protect so why not simply destroy the letters and sell the rings?

"Martha? You out here?"

"Yes, dear. Veggie garden."

She wanted to talk to Thomas about her thoughts. Of everyone, he was the person who knew the most of Frannie's day-to-day life. How she ran the house. Whether she kept personal possessions locked away, even from him. Who were her friends when they were married?

Martha tossed off her gardening gloves and rubbed her eyes. She wouldn't speak with him. To hear of his life with her best friend... her shoulders slumped.

Your own fault for leaving River's End.

Her biggest flaw was her temper. Certainly back then. Temper and stubborn pride. On more than one occasion, Tom had promised he'd help her control both once they married. Well, now they were finally married, she'd learnt to control them herself.

"What are we planting now?" Thomas arrived with two cups of steaming coffee. "Ready for a break?"

"Good morning. Thank you and yes. Shall we sit?"

Thomas led the way to the bench under their favourite tree, waited until Martha sat, and joined her. "This is hot, so be careful."

"I'm hardly a child!" So much for controlling herself.

"Then, there's no need to react like one." His voice was calm, but his eyes glinted with something Martha hadn't seen for so very long. "Perhaps if you are over-tired, you should reconsider the late nights."

She leaned back against the tree, eyes never leaving his face despite the warmth creeping through her body. "I didn't intend to sound sharp. And I'm not over-tired."

"Then, what's on your mind?"

The coffee tasted good and drinking it gave Martha time to think, and now stare into its depths. She could feel Thomas watching her. "We don't have a present for Christie and Martin."

He chuckled. "And that's why you snapped at me?"

"Sorry. It is one of many things on my mind. Do you know what we should get them, because I've exhausted my ideas."

"A puppy. Then they can give Randall to us."

"Or you can get a puppy."

"Which will dig up your garden... although you were doing a good job of it yourself."

"Something for their house. Or garden."

"Let's see." Thomas put his cup onto the seat at his side and counted on his fingers. "Daphne and John gave them a greenhouse for their wedding. Angus and Elizabeth provided a gift card from the nursery in Green Bay. Barry's gift was a voucher for when they need more fencing. Sylvia and family gave those lovely matching vases. Think we might need something less domestic."

"Shall we go shopping then?"

"After breakfast. I'll get started."

"We might as well book the holiday for Elizabeth and Angus whilst we're out, as long as you still think it is okay?"

Thomas stood, and offered a hand to Martha. "If they don't want it, we'll take it." He pulled her onto her feet, and kissed her forehead. "See you inside. Follow the smell of fresh toast."

She watched him wander back across the grass and through the wrought iron gate, carrying their cups. Their life together was precious, more so because of the years apart.

You can't rake over the past with him.

He had issues forgiving Frannie already. It would be cruel to bring up so many old memories.

10

JAG

*N*ot long after breakfast, and before he and Elizabeth could have their planned chat over a cup of tea, Angus was phoned by John Jones. He'd taken the call in his bedroom, not at all certain he wanted to hear John's news, but there it was. The owners of the property they'd discussed would consider leasing it to Angus short term. They arranged a time to meet and now, here Angus was, waiting for his friend.

He'd driven down the overgrown driveway to park near a garage. He sat for a while, mind darting all over as he thought through his options.

Stay at Palmerston House as a paid guest as he'd been for some months.

Accept Elizabeth's request for him to stay but not as a paying guest.

Or move.

He had to do something, for he couldn't bear for anyone to think poorly of the dear woman who'd become much more to him than a friend.

Many years ago he'd been married and so happily. As had Elizabeth to her Keith. But both marriages ended with the sad loss of a partner, and they'd become accustomed to living alone. Until he'd arrived to visit Christie, and pretty much stayed ever since. There was no denying the immediate delight he and Elizabeth took in each other's company.

Between all the dramas this past year in River's End, their relationship strengthened, but when he was injured by Elizabeth's guest, Bernie Cooper, she'd blamed herself. Much as she tried to pretend everything was okay, Angus knew it still bothered her. Perhaps it was best he moved into a place of his own for a while, so he could properly court her.

John's car drew up behind and Angus climbed out of his. John already looked overheated in his too-tight suit and tie. He wiped his forehead as he closed the door. "Be a warm one today."

They shook hands. "Think we might have a storm later."

"As long as it cools things down. Right, let's have a look through." John led Angus to the front of the house and up several steps. "Been for sale for a couple of years. I cleaned it up a bit after Bernie Cooper camped out here. Crushed, empty water bottles all over the place." He unlocked the door and pushed it open for Angus to go through. "Warn you though, it isn't Palmerston House."

Stale air was replaced by the unpleasant stench of wet carpet as Angus stepped into a dark hallway and almost put his foot straight into a hole in the floorboards.

John grabbed his arm. "Whoops, steady on." He took his phone out and found its flashlight app, shining it around. There was rotting further along, and the first room showed signs of water damage. "Owners won't spend anything on it. Roof must be full of holes. Sorry, Angus, this isn't even habitable."

Back in the sunshine, door locked, John shook his head. "I'll keep looking for you."

"Thank you, John."

They returned to the cars. "Not my business, but I'm surprised Elizabeth is okay with you moving out. Not as though there isn't plenty of room there."

"I've yet to mention it to her."

"She'll find out on her own if you look at enough places. Small town talk and all that. Might hurt her feelings."

Angus agreed. As John backed down the driveway, he formulated the conversation they needed to have. It would start with a declaration of his love, and then how deeply he respected her. From there, he knew they'd talk through any concerns she might have. He put his hand on the car door.

There was sound near the garage. A rustle. There was no breeze, so it must be a rabbit or the like. But then, a whimper. Head tilted to listen, Angus watched the bushes. A few branches moved, and a black nose poked out, sniffed the air, and then retreated.

"It is quite safe to show yourself." Nothing. "Very well, if you're hungry, I can arrange some food, but you need to come out."

Back at the car, he opened the front passenger door. In the glove box was an unopened packet of plain biscuits. A leftover of his last long drive several months ago.

The moment he opened the packet near the front of the car, the nose reappeared through the branches. "Probably not an ideal offering, but I'd like to meet you." He placed a biscuit on the ground and stepped back.

Like a black streak, a dog raced over, picked up the biscuit, and returned to the bushes. Once the sound of crunching stopped, Angus took a second biscuit but this time, held it out. "Come on, I like dogs."

Hesitant at first, the dog crept toward Angus, eyes flicking between his face and the biscuit. When the dog would take the whole thing, Angus held on, letting the dog chew pieces off. Last morsel devoured, the dog backed off, but with an expression of hope.

"How long since you've eaten?" The dog was a kelpie, bred to work sheep. This one was thin, his ribs obvious beneath a dirty coat. "You may have one more, then perhaps you'll join me in the car and we can get you a proper meal." The dog's ears pricked up and down, then the very tip of his tail wagged as Angus offered another biscuit. There was a tag on the dog's collar with the name 'Jag' on it.

"Jag. Is this you?"

The dog sat, his tail thumping the ground.

Angus opened the passenger door. "Well, Jag, would you care to jump in?"

11

FEARS CONFIRMED

*A*n hour after Angus returned – with a scrawny, hungry dog in tow – Elizabeth was as on edge as she could ever remember. Jag was well mannered and waited with wide eyes as she found some meat scraps and a bowl whilst Angus filled the water bucket they kept for Randall's visits. He'd eaten quickly, run outside briefly and returned with an expectant glance at the fridge that made her laugh. With no more food forthcoming, he'd curled up under the kitchen table and slept.

"Is there a phone number on the tag?" she'd asked as she made a fresh pot of tea. The one she'd prepared much earlier this morning went cold when Angus suddenly left after a phone call.

"There is, but the number is disconnected. I hate the thought of him going to the pound though."

"Well, I'm sure if we let Trev know the phone number he can chase it up rather than call a ranger. Jag is quite safe here for the moment."

"How kind-hearted you are, Elizabeth." Angus took teacups from the cupboard.

I don't feel it.

No, she felt as though something important was out of her reach.

Until the other day when Belinda and George visited to play

Scrabble, her world was almost perfect. Christmas was near and she couldn't wait to give Angus the gift she'd found for him. In the moments at night as she fell asleep, her mind often drifted to what might be. A proposal. Another marriage to another wonderful man. How could one woman be so blessed in love?

But, as she'd returned to the living room, Angus words drifted out. "I shall move out as soon as possible." She'd stopped in her tracks, unable to comprehend what he meant. When she'd pulled herself together enough to follow Belinda in, he'd smiled and taken her hand as though nothing had happened.

"Where would you like your tea? Here, or by the pond?"

"Oh. Here is fine, Angus."

Last night he'd wined and dined her with no mention of his plan to leave. Her request for him to stay as a non-paying guest remained unanswered. The phone call this morning sent him to his room, then off in his car with almost no explanation. Now, her hands shook as she poured tea.

They sat at one corner of the kitchen table, Jag still asleep. He needed a bath, his coat was so dirty and he smelt as though he'd been neglected for a long time. But he was content and could wait a little longer.

"The tea is lovely, just the way I like it." Angus smiled over his teacup.

Elizabeth barely tasted it. Any moment he would tell her the past months being so close were in her imagination. Tension coiled inside her and she put her cup down.

Angus didn't seem to notice. "I did enjoy dinner last night. And I have thought about your sweet offer for me to stay without payment."

Underneath the table, Elizabeth curled her hands into balls. "I... I meant it, Angus."

"Thank you, dear lady. But it wouldn't be right for me to take such advantage of you."

Jag stirred, touching Elizabeth's feet. "Where did you find him? The dog?"

"Just outside town."

"On the road?"

He shook his head. "Actually, no. At the property for sale. The one that's been on the market for so long."

She could barely force the words out. "Why were you there?"

"I should have spoken sooner. Elizabeth, please don't misunderstand my motives, but I think it is prudent for me to find my own place."

"You're not happy here."

"Elizabeth, quite the—" His phone rang. He pulled it from a pocket to reject the call and Elizabeth saw it was John Jones. She stood. "Please, let's talk about this." Angus held out his hand.

With a shake of her head, she picked up her teacup and walked to the sink.

"Elizabeth."

"Call John back. I'm sure it is important."

She felt Angus behind her.

Don't touch me. Please, please don't make this harder.

"Tell him you'll take it, if it's what you want."

"I'd like to explain myself. Can we sit?"

"No. You pack, dear. I understand completely. And it is for the best." Without a backward glance, she stumbled from the kitchen and to the back door. Angus called her name, but she had to keep going. Before he saw the silly tears or she made a real fool of herself by begging him to reconsider.

12

STORMY SKIES

*C*hristie and Martin wandered hand in hand along the tide line. Ahead, Randall rolled in an interesting smell, his legs kicking the air and satisfied grunts coming from his throat. Out along the horizon, storm clouds built and a warm wind stirred up the waves.

"I'm so proud of how well the salon is going, but being selfish, I'm also very happy to have you to myself unexpectedly." Martin lifted her hand to his lips. "Pity about the storm, or we could have sailed."

"This is nice. I am a bit concerned about Elizabeth though."

"For cancelling her appointment with you?"

"Belinda took the call and said she sounded strange."

"Belinda is prone to exaggeration."

They passed Randall, who leapt up and shook sand everywhere. Further along, the jetty was under siege from increasing waves, and they stopped to watch.

"There's something beautiful in the power of those waves." Martin put his arm around Christie's shoulders. "No wonder Thomas loves painting them."

"Well, the jetty has a lot to answer for. Bringing Thomas and Martha together and then almost killing her when she slipped off it."

"She shouldn't have been on it during a storm."

"Well, thank goodness Thomas went in after her. How frightening for them both."

"And for you, sweetheart, when you tied up *Jasmine Sea* here to look for me."

"Actually, tying her up was a relief. I thought the nightmare was over. It was when I came back and Derek tried to get back on board..."

Martin turned Christie in his arms and tilted her chin up. "The best memory I have is proposing to you, right on the end of the jetty." She relaxed against him. "Even though you stormed off at one point."

"Sorry. Ryan family temper."

"I've never seen Martha show it."

"It's there. Our wild Irish heritage."

He kissed her, then glanced at the sky. "Storm's getting close. Let's go home."

Randall trotted behind them as they climbed the narrow track up the cliff. At the top, they watched the black clouds rolling in, lightning flashing within their laden forms. The wind picked up, swirling Christie's hair around. "I might phone Belinda and tell her just to lock up when she's done and go home. I'll clean in the morning."

With the first long rumble of thunder, they followed Randall to the house. Rain splattered the sliding door as Martin unlocked it. "There goes my plan for a barbecue," he commented as Christie went inside ahead of him. "Seems it will be an intimate dinner for two instead. Candles, flowers, and—"

"Chocolate mousse?"

"I was going to say wine."

"That'll do. I'll quickly ring Belinda."

As Christie spoke to Belinda, the rain became a deluge, punctuated by thunder. Randall stared out through the sliding glass door, head tilting from side to side.

"Forget it, dog. Why don't you curl up on your bed?"

Randall glanced at Martin and whined, then pressed his nose against the rain-streaked glass.

"What is he doing?" Christie finished her call and frowned at Randall. "It's like he can hear something. Randall, what's up?"

He stiffened, and then his tail started to wag.

Martin headed back to the door, just as a figure appeared on the other side. A soaking wet figure carrying a bedraggled black dog.

---

*I*n dry clothes from Martin's wardrobe, Angus sat in the living room with a cup of coffee. Christie had towelled Jag down and he lay near the sliding door with Randall watching him from his bed. They'd sniffed and wagged tails earlier and now just kept an eye on each other.

Overhead the storm still bellowed, and it fitted the state of his mind. And heart.

Elizabeth.

Her final words had stopped him following her to the garden, where she'd disappeared from view toward the pond. "It is for the best."

"Angus? Is there anything I can get for you? Anything I can do?" Christie joined him on the sofa and put an arm around him.

"Letting us be here is plenty."

"But why—"

"Sweetheart, let Angus settle in before bombarding him with questions." Martin brought a coffee to Christie and sat opposite with his own. "Stay as long as you need to."

"Thank you, but I don't mind. After all, I've appeared here in the middle of a storm and with a strange dog. Thank goodness Randall is so accepting."

"Was he lost? Jag?"

"Yes, Christie. I discovered him hiding in some bushes at the house for sale out of town."

"Poor baby. Is there a phone number?"

"Disconnected. I'll let Trev know and see if he can track down the owner. Don't want him put in a pound."

"He's so thin. Oh, shall we feed him?" Christie began to get up and Angus put a hand on her arm.

"He's been fed. Elizabeth... she found him some meat earlier." Angus saw the question in Christie's eyes and sighed. "I've moved out of Palmerston House."

"What! Why?"

"A misunderstanding. Rather a big one, I fear." Jag appeared at Angus' side and rested his head on his knee. "I found this one because I was hoping to rent the house."

"Rent it? I really don't understand."

"Nor does Elizabeth. But I couldn't go on living there. Letting people think... well, believe I would take advantage of her."

"Okay, I have no idea what you mean, because nobody would think that! You're a paying guest, for goodness sake."

"But one who also loves the owner of the house."

Martin nodded. "I understand."

"Well, I don't."

Angus managed a smile. "I didn't wish her to feel... obliged, to share the home she created with Keith, should I propose."

Christie looked from Angus to Martin. "Is this a man thing?"

Martin raised an eyebrow. "It is an honour thing."

"Well, I think it is nice to be noble and all that, but unnecessary. Surely Elizabeth has some say in this?"

She did.

And she'd said it.

Christie continued. "After the storm, let's go to Palmerston House with a bottle of wine, and sort this all out."

If only it was so easy. For hours, Angus had driven aimlessly around River's End, Jag happy to sit in the footwell of the car. He'd stopped at the motel, but it was full for the holidays. He'd considered looking in Warrnambool and Green Bay but his heart yearned for his room in Palmerston House and the lady who had his heart. When the storm closed in, something brought him to his dear Christie and her husband.

"I know you mean well, Christie, but I'm not certain this can be sorted out, as you put it."

She opened her mouth to answer, but Angus saw her exchange a look with Martin and she refrained from answering. Instead, she held his hand.

13

A PROPERTY TO SELL

*E*lizabeth stood outside the real estate agency the next morning, waiting for Daphne to turn the 'Closed' sign to 'Open'. The rain from last night was gone, replaced by a cooler day with brilliant sunshine. Her hands gripped her handbag. She hadn't slept. Nor had she done what every instinct told her to do – phone Angus. At least she knew he was staying with Christie and Martin, thanks to a text message from Christie. He was safe.

"Well, hello there!" Daphne swung the door wide open with a smile. "What brings you by so early? I can put the kettle on if you'd like a cup?"

"Actually, Daphne, I'm here to see John. If he's in."

"You are? Oh, of course, come on in and I'll fetch him."

Once they were both inside, Daphne hurried behind the counter and picked up a phone. "I'll let him know you're waiting."

"Daph, I'm right here. Hello, Elizabeth." John came through the door from the kitchen. "Is everything alright?"

Nothing is right.

"I'd like to speak with you about property sales."

John's expression changed, Elizabeth was certain. He thought she was coming to ask about Angus. "About the value of properties in the area."

"Are you wanting to invest, Elizabeth?" Daphne came back around the counter. "John has some houses for sale in the new estate. Great for holiday rentals."

"No, I'm not interested in an investment property, Daphne, but thank you." She turned her gaze on John. "Nor am I interested in rentals."

"Er, I can't discuss... I mean, when someone comes to me as a client I must keep their confidence."

"John? Whatever are you talking about?" Daphne clearly knew nothing about John's arrangement with Angus. A small chunk of ice melted inside Elizabeth. She'd thought her friend knew all about Angus' desire to move out and hadn't told her. Perhaps things weren't as bad as she'd imagined. And during the long, lonely hours of the night, she'd imagined a lot.

"The fact is, I want to know how to sell a property. What is the procedure and how long does it take?"

Daphne and John turned wide eyes on her. It would be comical if it wasn't so serious. She'd never considered how everyone would react.

"Process is simple. We talk through expectations, value the property, plan a campaign to promote it – once I know what a client wants I do the work. But as for how long?" John scratched his head. "It depends, Elizabeth."

"On what?"

"Quality of the property in question. Demand from buyers. Asking price. Really, there are plenty of variables and sometimes a property holds such high appeal it sells even as it's listed."

"Well, I wish to sell a property and hope you'll do everything to make it happen quickly."

The office became so silent Elizabeth could hear the ticking of the clock behind the counter.

Take a breath.

She did. And planted her feet more firmly to keep her steady as she said the words she never expected to say.

"John. Daphne. I intend to sell Palmerston House and want you to do it for me."

"There you go, Elizabeth, and I've popped one of my homemade gingerbread cookies on the side. Being Christmas and all." Daphne put a cup and saucer on a coaster on John's desk. "Sure you don't want another, doll?"

"Fine, thank you, Daph. Would you close the door on the way out?"

Close the door?

Daphne almost said it aloud, but one look at Elizabeth's set face and she did as John asked. They never closed doors here, but then again, if Elizabeth wanted to keep this confidential for now, they couldn't risk anyone overhearing details.

If only she could hear the conversation though. Elizabeth was a dear friend and obviously quite upset about this decision. Daphne made herself a coffee, adding a cookie for a bit of a pick-me-up.

She hurried to her chair when the phone rang, answering with a small gasp, "River's End Real Estate, this is Daphne."

"Good morning, Daphne. This is Angus McGregor."

"Angus! How nice to hear from you. How may I help?" Was he meant to be in the meeting with John and Elizabeth? Not that he was an owner, but perhaps as support for Elizabeth.

"Would John be available for a quick word?"

"Well, actually not at this moment. He is with... umm, a client. May I take a message?"

"I see. Perhaps you would be kind enough to let him know things can wait until after Christmas."

Daphne wrote on a notepad. "Things can wait until after Christmas. Angus, will he understand this or should I provide further information?"

"He's welcome to phone me if he doesn't. On my mobile only, if you'd make a note."

"On your mobile only. Okay, all done."

"Thank you. I'll… I'll speak with you both later."

As she replaced the phone, she reread the note. "Things can wait until after Christmas. Can phone but only on mobile." Why? Were the phones down at Palmerston House? Maybe the storm affected them. "What assistance?" The other day, after waiting over at the bakery for ages as Sylvia made John's strange lunch, she'd finally come back just as Angus was leaving. He'd waved with a smile and John said they'd been talking about Christmas.

"But we're not all together for Christmas, unless he means at Christie and Martin's night?" Something wasn't right. Daphne didn't like secrets, unless they were the good type. If John was making things up, she'd get to the bottom of it. She bit into the cookie.

14

SEARCHING FOR ANSWERS

*S*ince unlocking the front door before eight this morning, Christie was on the go with clients, phone calls, and more clients. The hairdryer hummed, Belinda chattered non-stop, and the coffee machine got a thorough workout. It was a happy, relaxed environment for the client, based on Christie's past career in specialist make-up. On a film set, one needed to concentrate, work quickly and efficiently, and be calm. And it worked here also, particularly with the pre-Christmas rush.

When a brief lull gave Belinda and Lana – the new hairdresser – a chance to catch up with cleaning and prepping for the next clients, Christie ran over to the bakery and ordered morning tea. John was in line ahead of her and they chatted about the storm last night.

As they waited for their orders, she gave him a smile. "I'm on the trail of a small mystery, John."

"Should River's End be concerned?"

"Not this time. Really, it is tying up loose ends and I've got some of it sorted out, but need your help." She laughed at John's expression. "Just a couple of questions and they're about Palmerston House so should be easy."

The moment she mentioned Palmerston House, John's eyes flicked away and his lips tightened. What was that about? "Elizabeth suggested I speak with you."

"Elizabeth did? When was that?"

"Months ago. Is everything okay, John? You look worried."

"Do I? No, not at all. Please, what do you need to know? Although I suspect I won't have answers."

"Okay, as you know, we have a nineteenth century timber trunk at the cottage. The one I found with Thomas' letters to Martha inside."

John nodded, and ran a finger inside his collar.

"The trunk came from Palmerston House. Martha recalls it being in Gran's bedroom. So, we're trying to discover how – when – the trunk was moved."

"It wasn't me. Promise." His laugh came out like a cough.

"No, but you handled the sale of Palmerston House."

"How do you know? I'm sorry. I meant, yes I did. Back then."

"Well, that's the only time it's ever been for sale. Do you remember Gran visiting? Did she come to River's End to take anything before it sold to Elizabeth and Keith?"

"She did spend a few days here, at Palmerston House, but I have no idea what she did. A reclusive lady, Dorothy Ryan was. Kept to herself unless she wanted something."

Christie's mouth curved up a little. "You have a good memory, John. She was exactly like you say."

"Order's ready, John!" Sylvia called from the counter.

"Sorry I can't be more helpful, Christie."

"Thanks anyway."

John collected his order and nodded to Christie as he walked past. Near the door he turned around, and came back. "You know, this might not mean anything, but I do remember your Gran visiting George. And seeing his car at Palmerston House around the same time. Of course, my memory might be wrong."

Or it might be right.

Christie watched him leave, then collected her own order, deep in thought.

"*W*ho knows how long the poor fellow was on his own, but he can't get enough to eat." Angus sat on one side of a desk in the police station, Jag under his feet.

Across from him was Senior Constable Trevor Sibbritt, River's End's only police officer and long-time resident. He had Jag's tag in one hand and the mouse for his computer in the other.

"Pretty sure I know where he's from, but he's come a long way."

"It would be wonderful to find his home."

"Might be a problem with it." Trev clicked a few times, then frowned. "As I thought."

"What's wrong?"

"I thought I recognised him and the phone number looked familiar. Comes from the other side of the mountain. Probably a good twenty kilometres across country so no wonder he's thin."

"Can we phone his owner? Is there another way to find them?"

"Unfortunately not, Angus. His owner passed away a couple of months ago. Neighbour from the next farm found him. Just old age, poor guy. He didn't even run sheep anymore, just him and Jag all alone on a big block of land."

"How terrible. But nobody found the dog with him? Next of kin?"

Trev shook his head. "Guess we'll have to take Jag to the pound and see if a home comes along."

"Is it necessary? I mean, what if someone was to offer a home now?"

"There's a process. Might be able to speak to someone though. Pound tends to fill up this time of year. Are you offering to take him? Elizabeth okay with him staying?"

Angus glanced at Jag. "Christie and Martin are okay with keeping him for a bit. We actually have someone in mind, but haven't spoken to them yet."

"Right, well you take him back to them for now and I'll make some calls."

15

DEADLY MEMORIES

The jangle of the door cut through George's thoughts. He straightened up on his stool behind the long, glass counter, surprised to see Martha. She rarely visited him here, and he couldn't recall having a private conversation with her since... well, since she and Thomas were engaged the first time.

"Martha, what brings you here today? Christmas shopping?" George pushed himself off the stool.

"Hello, George. Please, sit down if you prefer. I will do some shopping whilst I'm here, but hoped to ask you something first. If you don't mind."

"Ask away. But I will sit again, if you really don't think me rude. Old bones."

"Our bones may be old, but our minds are still young. So Tom keeps telling me." Martha smiled her sweet smile and George knew it wouldn't be difficult to imagine all of them back in their youth. His heart beat a bit faster, wishing himself into his younger body.

"Christie and I are determined to find out how the trunk got to the attic. She wanted to drop by to see you again but is so busy with her lovely salon, so I'm here instead. About the letters, and my rings."

George put both hands on his legs to stop a sudden tremor.

Not this. Let it go.

A lifetime of secrets needed to stay protected. For everyone's sake, not only his. He leaned forward a little.

"As I told Christie, Frances wanted to sell the rings. I insisted she return them to Thomas."

"And I thank you for doing so. You didn't answer her question about the trunk though. The letters."

"What about them? They were written by Thomas and sent to you. But Dorothy intercepted them. It's quite common knowledge now."

"Christie told you Dorothy kept them, but did she say Frannie wanted them?"

The strangest sensation clutched George inside his stomach, creeping to his chest. "Christie... did not tell me." Martha was watching him with an expression he'd seen before. She was sizing him up, working out if he was being honest.

Martha extended her left hand. "You made these rings out of love, dear George. Love for Thomas. He always looked up to you, counted on you to keep him grounded when his life ran out of control. Like with his father. You are a good man, George."

"Except I kept the grandfather clock for decades to fulfil my family's promise to Henry Temple."

"And returned it to Palmerston House when the time was right." Martha dropped her hand, her stare unnerving George. "But hiding a clock is one thing. Hiding love letters from your best friend to the woman he loved are quite another."

She knows. How can she know?

His jaw ached. When did it start to hurt? He clenched and unclenched it. "This has been a bad week, Martha. I may have unwittingly encouraged Angus to move out of Palmerston House."

"What? Oh dear, well, this is something else we can talk about, but please George, I've waited too long to know the truth, and I do believe you're the key to finding out."

He moved his hands to the counter as though to support himself. Except he was still sitting.

"George, Frannie was my best friend. I knew you adored her and I fully expected you to marry her one day. Is it possible you kept caring for her, even after she married Tom? That you'd have done anything for her?"

"Not that. I'd never have hidden those letters, Martha. Not from Thomas, nor you." He drew in a ragged breath. All this upset was making it harder to breathe. But he couldn't allow Thomas to believe he'd have been party to the terrible conspiracy. "There isn't much to tell. But I will, so you'll let me rest."

"Oh, George, I'm not meaning to distress you, dear. Please, go and rest and we can talk another time." Martha put her hand on his arm, alarm in her eyes.

"No. Now, or it's never. I don't wish to revisit the past ever again. Not for you, or Christie, or even Thomas, so mark my words and then it's done." There was a curious ache in his shoulder and tingling down his arm. He needed to lay down. Let his blood pressure settle with a nice glass of whiskey.

"Dorothy came to River's End twice after you left. The first time she took the rings from Frances. But I didn't know this until much later. Until she was selling Palmerston House."

----

*1*993
It took George a few seconds to recognise the woman across the counter. Dressed in black pants and jacket, hair wound tightly in a bun, expensive and quite beautiful jewellery on her hands and neck, it was her stern face he remembered.

"Miss Ryan. You're back in River's End."

"Clearly. As soon as you close the shop today, come to Palmerston House. The back door will be open but knock first. Tell nobody."

"I beg your pardon? Why do you want me to do this?"

"I have a small errand for you to take care of, and no-one else in this town is suitable."

"Miss Ryan, with all respect, if you require assistance at Palmerston

House I am happy to help, but do require more information than to just turn up and tell nobody! Is this a... legal... errand?"

"It doesn't matter. You'll be there."

"It does matter."

"For goodness sake. You'll transport a small trunk to the old stationmaster's cottage. Once there, put it in the attic and lock the place back up."

This was getting stranger by the minute. "Why?"

"It is none of your business! You'll do this and then you will forget you did this. If I could manage it myself I would, but I'm not strong enough. So, you will."

"Actually, I won't. I'm sorry, but—"

"But?" she snarled, leaning over the counter. "George Campbell, my mother knew about the grandfather clock." She stabbed a finger in the direction of the clock in the corner. "It was stolen from Palmerston House before my ancestor took possession and your family have been keeping it for generations. Now, I don't know why and don't care at all, but I will not hesitate to contact the police and every person in this town if you refuse to help me. Understand?"

---

*G*eorge had understood. "I did as she said. The trunk was locked so I never knew what was inside. I took it into the attic and pushed it into the farthest corner."

Martha had her hand over her mouth.

His chest was so tight and heavy. "Forgive me, Martha. I didn't know." He gripped the counter to stop himself falling from the stool.

"George. I'm going to get some help. Are you okay to sit there?"

He couldn't answer. There was no air in his lungs and his legs wouldn't work. He felt Martha's hands on his arms.

"George! Somebody, help us!"

16

HOSPITAL

*I*n Green Bay hospital, Christie sat beside Martha, who gripped her hand as they waited for news about George. Thomas paced. Up and down the hallway to the doors George had been wheeled through, then around the seats in the middle of the waiting room.

Martin sat opposite the women, head in his hands. Christie longed to reach out to him, but Martha had hold of her too tightly. He'd barely spoken since arriving at the jewellery shop a moment after she had. People were milling around in there, John and Daphne, Sylvia, and there was little room to move.

"Let me through." Martin had reached George and sat him against the wall, gently straightening each leg out. He'd partly fallen, partly sunk to the ground and Martha had struggled to move him from the difficult tangle he'd landed in. "You need to be upright, George. Is it your heart?"

In too much pain to answer, George had managed to nod. Christie covered him with a blanket from the back room, then ushered everyone but Martin and Martha out. "Keep an eye out for the ambulance. Can someone please go and get Thomas?"

The ambulance arrived before Thomas, and it was Martin who rode to the hospital with George.

"This is all my fault," Martha murmured. She'd barely spoken since they'd arrived, nor touched the water Christie gave her.

"Oh, Auntie, how could it be?"

"I upset him. I forced him to remember things he didn't want to."

"What do you mean?" Thomas stopped pacing. "What things?"

"About the... the trunk."

"Our trunk?"

Martha nodded.

"Why were you asking him? Are you doing what I said not to do and looking for answers about it, Martha?"

"You didn't say I couldn't." She raised her chin. "In fact, all you said was perhaps it was better left alone."

"It was what I meant." Thomas stared at Martha and she met his eyes, not backing down.

"Stop it, both of you." Martin stood. "This is why I stay out of other people's affairs. And I should never have agreed to help you with this either, Thomas." He glanced at Christie. "Do I need to ask if you were involved in what Martha's doing?"

"Are you admitting to helping Thomas with a mystery?"

Martin stalked to the end of the hallway. After a moment of silence, Thomas sighed and followed him.

Christie watched them stare through the windows in the doors, then Thomas put an arm around Martin's shoulders. She squeezed Martha's hand. "Everyone is overwrought. Things will settle down once we know how George is."

"I shouldn't have pushed him. He told me it was too painful, but I wanted to know."

"Did he tell you anything?"

A range of emotions crossed Martha's face. Sadness, anger, and then back to worry. "It was all Dorothy—"

"Martha, Christie? Oh, is there any news? What happened?" Elizabeth hurried from the elevator and sat beside them. "Daphne is beside herself but John insisted she not come with me."

"Why would he do that?" Martha asked. "But there's no news yet. We're all so worried."

Thomas and Martin came back, both calmer but their faces still etched with concern. Christie stood so Thomas could sit beside Martha, which he did, with a quick kiss to her cheek.

At last Christie was able to go to Martin, and she put her arms around his waist, leaning against his chest. Tension kept him rigid, but he held her against him. There were no words. George meant so much to Martin, not only as his godfather, but the other man in his life growing up. It was George who he bought *Jasmine Sea* from years ago, long before her name change. There was a powerful connection between them.

"Elizabeth, thanks for being here." Thomas leaned back in his seat. "Is Angus parking the car?"

"Oh!" Christie exhaled and Martin released her. "Umm, Thomas—"

"It is fine," Elizabeth took a deep breath, "well, not fine. Angus has moved out of Palmerston House." She tried very hard to smile, but her lips ended up firmly planted together.

Thomas reached across Martha and patted her hand. "Well, it won't be for long. No matter what happened, there's always a way back."

The door at the end of the hallway opened and, as one, Thomas, Martha, and Elizabeth stood. Martin stepped forward as the doctor headed their way. "How's George, doctor?"

"Yup. Look, he's conscious and breathing on his own. Still waiting for some results back but he's suffered a cardiac incident. He needs to stay on his medication, which he hasn't been taking for a while."

"What medication?"

"Not something I can go into. Does he have a relative here?"

"I'm his godson. He doesn't have anyone but us," Martin said. "Thomas is his closest friend."

"Right. He's been asking for someone though. Mind you, he is disoriented, but he asked me to find Frances."

The colour drained from Thomas' face and he opened his mouth as though to speak, then closed it again.

The doctor glanced at his watch. "I take it Frances isn't here? One of you can sit with him for a while, just one."

"I'll go. I'm Frances' grandson." Martin glanced toward Thomas, who turned and stalked toward the elevator. Martha trailed him, her shoulders slumped.

"Go, Martin, I'll follow them." Christie forced a smile. "Thanks, doctor."

In a moment only Christie and Elizabeth remained. "Angus is okay, Elizabeth, but you two need to talk. Sorry to interfere, but please, don't leave it too late." Then she rushed after Thomas and Martha.

17

CABIN ON THE MOUNTAIN

*T*homas made it to his four wheel drive before Christie caught him. He knew Martha was somewhere behind, struggling to keep up, but nothing would stop him. His legs had a mind of their own and his brain fought to work out what just happened.

Don't think. Not yet.

He shoved his hand into a pocket for car keys.

"Thomas! Wait up."

Before he could fit the key in the lock, she was at his side, hand on his arm. He looked at her, puzzled. "Christie, why are you here?"

"You've had a shock. What if we let poor Martha catch up and we'll go find a coffee shop."

"Don't want coffee."

"That's not the point."

He stared past her at Martha, almost hobbling in her haste to reach him. Her eyes were wide and he was sure he saw tears. "There's something I need to do. I'll be back."

"Where are you—"

"Christie, no. I said I'll be back." He unlocked and opened the door. "Sorry. Tell her I'm sorry." Before anyone could stop him, he climbed inside and started the motor. As he pulled out of the parking spot, he glanced in the mirror and wished he hadn't. Martha was sobbing in Christie's arms. His foot lifted from the accelerator.

He asked me to find Frances.

That's what the doctor said. His foot went down again.

He drove toward River's End with almost no conscious thought. There was somewhere he had to go and he blinkered his thoughts. Shoved them into a bag and closed it. If he thought too hard, he'd change his mind.

Down the hill past the cottage, over the bridge, through town. He turned onto the road to the mountains, and glanced at the jewellery shop. It was more than a shop. A place he'd been welcomed by George's father, the previous jeweller, even to the point of living with them for a short while when things were too bad at home. Then George took over, and he created the beautiful rings now on Martha's finger. George gave Thomas the push to propose, and he'd laughed as he'd left with the ring box, telling his best friend it would be him he'd blame if he was heading for misery.

"How could we have known?" he muttered aloud, accelerating as the road opened up. The misery had come in volumes, thanks not to a marriage to Martha, but by the conspiracy of her sister, Dorothy, and his own future wife, Frannie. Frances. Did George never stop wishing for her? He shut it all out again.

Another twenty minutes passed until he slowed and took a dirt road. Despite the steely grip on the wheel, his heart lightened as the four wheel drive twisted its way higher and higher, through increasingly dense forest and over deteriorating ground. Huge potholes and a sheer drop on one side kept his focus on staying on the road and by the time he reached a narrow track, he was exhausted.

Not long now.

A steep incline, one final curve, and the landscape changed as he burst onto a small parcel of flat land with a cabin at its edge.

The moment the engine was off, he climbed out and stood, eyes closed, listening. Birdsong. Nothing else. Mountain air – thick with mid-afternoon heat – filled his senses. A deep breath in and he released it slowly.

Home.

He opened his eyes.

The cabin was never locked. Who would even know where to find it? Besides, most of his important possessions were now in the cottage, the one from his childhood. Inside, it was so much cooler but smelt musty. Thomas left the front door open. No point opening windows on such a short visit.

Need to come back. Bring Martha. And show Christie where Martin grew up.

He loved this place. Missed it more than he'd realised. There were some paintings on the walls he'd forgotten. One done by Martin. He gently took it off its hook and leaned it near the front door to take back.

At the door to his old bedroom he hesitated. Here he'd mourned Frannie. Mourned his son, Thomas, and daughter-in-law Anna.

He stepped in. The furniture was here, but little else. Thomas pulled a mat aside, revealing a floor safe. Originally installed to keep legal documents and money safe should fire threaten the cottage whilst he was away, he'd eventually put other items in it. Things he didn't know what else to do with.

Should be forgotten.

Well, forgetting hadn't worked. With a sigh, he sat on the floor.

On his key chain was the key to the safe. When he'd first seen the key to the trunk, it reminded him of this one. Both skeleton keys. Both belonging to something life changing. Christie's key opened both the trunk, and the stone door beneath Palmerston House that led to a tunnel to the sea. His key opened this safe. Old memories. And something he'd kept, even though he'd never known why.

Thomas opened the safe. At the top was a large envelope marked 'Martin's school photographs'. He chuckled, wondering if he should give it to Christie first, or Martin. Beneath this was a tin box, filled with cash. Old Australian notes, coins now out of circulation, and a thick wad of fifty dollar notes. He'd get something nice for Martha. Guilt flooded through him.

Never make her cry again.

She'd understand once she knew what he was doing.

Only one thing remained. A shoebox. Old. Tied with red, velvet ribbon.

Frannie's. He'd found it after the car accident. Long after the funeral for three, when he was dealing with a distressed, confused toddler. He knew it meant something to her for it was in her box of special things, along with her wedding dress, a piece of their wedding cake, and photographs he'd forgotten about. Some of him and Martha from the days when Frannie trailed behind, taking snapshots.

Somewhere in here were the answers. The ones Martha sought. And perhaps something to ease George's mind. For George was his best friend. No matter what.

18

HARSH WORDS

Martin eventually emerged from George's room, deep lines around his eyes.

"How is he?" Christie was the only person left in the waiting room. "Where is everyone?"

"Thomas took off somewhere. Martha was upset so Elizabeth drove her home. How's George?"

"Asleep." He ran a hand through his hair. "He is wired up to all sorts of things, but said he was comfortable. He knew me, knew where he was, so I don't know what happened earlier."

"Asking for Frannie?"

"He didn't mention her again. But he wants to see Thomas."

"Will the doctor let Thomas go in?"

With a shake of his head, Martin led the way to the elevator. "Not yet, but it doesn't matter anyway if he's not here."

Inside the elevator, Martin pulled Christie into his arms. "You should have gone home, sweetheart. Or back to work."

"Belinda and Lana have rescheduled a couple of clients. I'll do an evening later this week."

After kissing the top of Christie's head, Martin sighed. "Where's Thomas?"

"Last seen he was driving in the direction of River's End." Christie explained how Thomas drove off, although she'd pleaded with him to wait for Martha. "She's so hurt, Martin. But once she stopped crying, all I saw was anger in her eyes."

"They'll sort it out. Thomas said he needed to do something. He's probably back at the cottage by now. I'll call once we're on the way."

A few moments later, as Christie drove out of Green Bay, Martin hung up from leaving a voice mail for Thomas. "Tell me what you and Martha have been doing, please."

"There's not a lot to tell." Christie glanced at Martin's stern expression. "Martha is looking for closure. Finding out how the trunk got to the cottage might help, so she's been reading Dorothy's diary—"

"And this was worth George having a heart attack?"

Christie touched the brakes. "Don't."

"He's an old man. Being interrogated—"

"Martin! Nobody did such a thing!"

Breathe, Christie.

Martin was exhausted. Worried.

"We all love George, and the doctor said he hadn't been taking his medication. It isn't fair to blame Martha. Or me."

She drove for a few moments with no response from Martin, and she wasn't about to argue with him. Or even look at him. They needed to work together to support George, and be there for Thomas and Martha, not make things worse.

Martin's phone rang. "Thomas? Where are you?" He put it on speaker.

"Almost at River's End. Coming to the hospital."

"Well, there's no point, because the doctor said no more visitors today."

"But I've got something for him."

"Tomorrow. Have you been at the cabin?"

Christie shot a curious look at Martin. Why would he go there when his best friend was in hospital?

"Where's Martha? Is she with you?"

"Thomas, Martha went home. She was terribly upset by the way you left." Christie sped up a little. "You only had to a wait another minute and tell her what you were doing."

"And she'd have wanted to come with me. It wasn't her concern and it certainly isn't yours."

"Okay, Thomas. There's been enough upset for one day." Martin reached across and squeezed Christie's leg, leaving his hand there. "We'll meet you at the cottage in a few moments and I'll update you on George." He hung up.

"Did you just—"

"No point talking to him on the phone when he's in a mood." Martin put his phone in a pocket. "I shouldn't have said what I did to you, Christie. Sorry."

"I love you." She smiled at Martin and his own lips flickered up for a moment. Then he closed his eyes and leaned back.

When Christie drove down her old road a short while later, he opened them again with a start, then straightened. Outside the cottage, Angus' black Range Rover was on the grass verge. Christie parked behind it, leaving the driveway for Thomas once he arrived.

Angus was in the lounge room with Martha, Jag sitting at her side. She put her hand on his head as Christie and Martin came in. "He likes me."

"He does." Christie patted Jag and crouched beside Martha. "Have you spoken to Thomas yet?"

Martha's face hardened, only the flash in her eyes giving away deep emotions which Christie knew must be churning inside. "He seems to have better things to do than speak with me."

"Not true." Thomas stood at the doorway, holding the shoebox. "Had to go to the cabin."

Jags ears shot up and he stood, sniffing the air.

"Who's this?" Thomas' voice softened. Jag went to him, circled him once, and then leaned against his legs, staring up with an adoring gaze. Thomas scratched behind his ears. "Handsome boy."

"This is Jag," Angus said. "Found him the other day and he's staying with me until Trev finds out if he needs a home."

Martha pushed herself to her feet. "Whilst I appreciate you all dropping by, I'd like to speak to my husband now. I don't mean to sound rude."

"Of course." Angus got up. "Please update me on George's progress." He patted Thomas' shoulder on the way past. "Coming, Jag?" He headed down the hallway and, after licking Thomas' hand, the dog followed.

"Are you sure, Auntie?" Christie stood. Martha nodded. Martin held his hand out and she took it. "We're only a call away. Both of you." She levelled a look at Thomas but his eyes were on Martha.

---

*M*artha stared at Thomas until the back door closed. She glanced at the shoebox he still held, curious but overcome with confusing feelings of anger and something else she couldn't quite identify.

"Do you know how George is?" Thomas finally asked.

"After you drove off like that, I couldn't even go back upstairs. Christie asked Elizabeth to bring me home because she needed to stay with Martin. Like we should have."

"I needed to get this."

"A shoebox, Thomas?"

"It was Frannie's."

"You kept this? Even after—"

"After what, Martha?" Thomas took a step toward Martha, who didn't move. She couldn't. Her feet were frozen in place.

"Us."

"Us? This isn't about us."

"We married and you kept Frannie's things. Her mementos? Pictures of you both?" As her voice raised, she saw the warning glint in Thomas' eyes but ignored it. "You won't even talk about her. About what happened to make you want to marry her, and now I see this?"

"Stop, Martha. Stop before we both say things we shouldn't."

"What? That I ruined everything by running away in the first place? It was all my fault? Or how it took less than a few months for—"

"No more. This isn't about you."

Before Martha could say another word, he was gone. Storming out through the front door.

With a jolt, she recognised the odd feeling she'd had. Betrayal.

19

TO THE JETTY

*a*t the gate, Christie, Martin, and Angus talked, the black kelpie standing nearby. They all looked at Thomas as he closed the door in his wake and strode past, clutching the shoebox.

"Thomas?"

"Going for a walk, son."

"Granddad—"

"Stay out of it." He didn't intend to sound abrupt. Martin wasn't the problem, nor the others, but he wasn't about to stop for chit-chat. He realised the dog was beside him.

Jag.

"Go on, back to Angus."

"I'll pick him up later," Angus called from the gate.

"Fine, but don't expect conversation," Thomas told Jag, who didn't appear concerned.

His heart told him to stop, take a few deep breaths, and turn around. He loved Martha beyond life. But his head sent him away. How could she say those things? Did she really believe he'd chosen Frannie over her? Kept this... this box of hers to remember a woman who tricked him into marriage?

At the end of the street, Thomas stopped only long enough to check for traffic, then crossed, Jag still at his side. It was late in the day and the air was finally cooling. He went through the graveyard, winding his way to the stone steps to avoid passing the three grave- stones of his family. He paused at the top of the steps to stare at the horizon.

Martha misses Ireland. What if she goes back?

Jag went on ahead, and he followed.

On the beach, he kicked off his shoes and walked to the tideline. Jag had already run to the waves and was chasing them, then running back to Thomas as they swept toward him.

As always, the jetty drew him and as he'd done so many times, for so many years, he trod its creaky old boards to the very end, where he lowered himself, feet dangling. The sea was too low to dip his feet in, but a fresh breeze was welcome. Jag lay at his side, staring down into the water, eyes darting around at the fish below.

"Where do you belong?" Thomas asked him, getting a wag of his tail in response. He took a good look at the dog. Too thin. Needed a few good meals and lots of brushing. But a fine dog, no doubt. Angus said he'd found him. He'd ask where. Another time.

Thomas put the shoebox down. Now it was more than the last of Frannie's secrets. It was the reason he was sitting here and not with his wife and family. All his suspicions about his friend's closely kept feelings for Frannie were true. He'd never stopped caring for her. And perhaps something inside this box would mean something.

Bit by bit, the anger and disappointment drained away. The shock of George's heart attack still coursed through him, but Thomas now recognised it played a large part of his earlier behaviour. Of course Martha would be hurt, him leaving the way he had at the hospital. Soon he'd go and see if he could repair the mess he'd made.

---

*H*e was there. Martha had taken a chance Thomas would go to his special place, their special place, but all the way here she'd second guessed herself. It was almost dusk, just light enough to see the stone steps as she took her time going down them. Her old ankle injury still made the steps a challenge, but nothing would stop her putting things right.

She made it as far as the beach end of the jetty before stopping for a rest. Jag noticed her and trotted over, interested in the picnic basket she'd put down. Thomas wasn't far behind.

Martha stood as straight as she could, her head high. No matter what he said, she'd stay strong and make sure he understood no disagreement would come between them again. His face was so stern.

Have I gone too far?

Thomas stopped beside the picnic basket, expression unchanging. Her heart pounded as he leaned down and picked it up.

He held out his other hand and she grabbed hold. By the time they reached the far end of the jetty, tears streamed down her face. Once he'd put the basket down, he turned to her, eyes narrowing as he saw her crying so silently.

"I promised you I'd help you learn how to control this temper of yours. Remember, we were up at the lookout and a night bird startled you?"

"Yes. And… and I remember you wanted to elope. We should have, Tom." A sob escaped her and he found a handkerchief, tenderly dabbing her eyes and cheeks, which only made the tears flow faster.

"If we'd eloped, there'd be no Martin. Nobody to marry Christie. No-one to care for Randall. Well, maybe me."

The sense of his words cut through the longing for a different past, and she nodded, gulping back the tears.

"And before you say it, I was wrong to take off to the cabin without a word but I wasn't even sure at first where I was going. I knew in the back of my mind there was something I could do to help George, but it wasn't until I was halfway there I realised why. I'd like to open this with you." He gestured to the shoebox, on the jetty beside the picnic basket.

"It is private."

"Secrets only hurt, my darling. No more, not if I can help it." Thomas wrapped his arms around Martha until she almost couldn't breathe. His familiar, beloved scent enveloped her and for the first time in hours, she was alive again. "No more raised voices. Okay?" Once she'd nodded, he released her.

Jag sniffed around the basket again.

"I'm thinking we should be opening this first. After all, you've gone to a lot of trouble."

"And a picnic is your favourite meal of the day?"

"Any meal with you is my favourite."

20

LOVE THEM AND LOSE THEM

*P*almerston House felt so lonely. From the first morning cup of tea, to a quiet drink out on the verandah as the sun set, everything reminded Elizabeth of Angus. He'd been gone for several days now, in fact, she knew exactly how many hours, if not minutes. Their paths almost crossed once. She'd dropped Martha at the cottage after George was admitted to hospital, and on her way home, he was driving up the hill as she drove down. Their eyes met for an instant and Elizabeth's heart jumped. Both kept driving and by the time she turned into the gates of Palmerston House, she was calm and resolute.

But this afternoon, for some reason, she yearned to see Angus. Every time she passed the Christmas tree, she expected to see him. And as she hurried past it now to answer the front door, her emotions got the better of her and she paused to wipe away a tear before letting Martha in.

"Sorry to be so long, Thomas wanted to check on George again first." Martha kissed Elizabeth's cheek. "Oh. Were you crying, dear?"

"No. Yes. A bit. Anyway, come in, I've made some gingerbread men."

"Gingerbread men? I haven't had one of those for... well, I can't recall how long."

Arm in arm, Elizabeth and Martha wandered to the kitchen.

"Thomas was welcome to visit."

"He'll be along. Had some errands to run."

Elizabeth put the kettle on as Martha settled at the table.

"Palmerston House looks so beautiful, Elizabeth. Reminds me of Christmas here growing up."

"They must have been grand affairs."

"Father opened the house to the town for Christmas lunch and we'd have people dropping by all day. Even Mother, who normally avoided contact with anyone except her 'set' as she called her friends, would enjoy the day. And then at night, the four of us would have a formal dinner in the small dining room. We even dressed up for it." Martha smiled.

"I never imagined it that way."

"Perhaps I should ask everyone to dress up for our Christmas dinner at the cottage?"

Busy making tea, Elizabeth didn't answer. Once she had two cups poured, she brought them to the table, then uncovered a plate revealing a dozen perfect gingerbread men.

"Well, these look delicious. Don't let Thomas see or he'll want the lot."

As she sat, Elizabeth managed a faint smile. "He's welcome to them. I'm baking rather a lot these days."

"So, do we all dress up for Christmas dinner?" Martha helped herself to a gingerbread man and bit into his leg with a grin.

"I've been thinking about it. The dinner. I'm not going to be very good company so—"

"So, what? Are you saying you won't celebrate with your oldest friend?" Now, the other leg disappeared into Martha's mouth.

"It might be better if I go and cook George dinner and stay to make sure he eats."

"George is going to Sylvia's. He's doing well, actually. Back up and about and quite determined to show the doctor he is capable of still running his shop."

"I was surprised he came home so quickly." Elizabeth picked up a gingerbread man, but merely looked at it.

"Well, it wasn't a heart attack after all and he responded well to the medication he was supposed to already be taking. I don't remember all the details, although Thomas will, but after three days the hospital was very happy with his condition."

Elizabeth still stared at the gingerbread man.

"It won't eat itself, dear. Perhaps you would fill me in on why Angus no longer lives here? I am sorry it has taken so long for us to be alone together, but please talk to me." Martha put a hand onto Elizabeth's. "It was a terrible shock at the hospital when you told us he'd moved out."

"As it was a shock to me overhearing him tell George he was going to go." Elizabeth sighed and turned sad eyes to Martha. "I don't really know why. But when he explained where he found Jag, he said it was prudent for him to find his own place."

"Prudent? I suppose if he wants to marry you, he'd rather propose on an even playing field."

"I don't understand."

Martha waved her arm around at the kitchen. "He's an old-fashioned gentleman, dear. You own this beautiful home and he lived here, as a guest. As much as it wouldn't matter to you if he was rich or a pauper, to him it would. Part of his code of honour, if you like."

"But... but I love him for him. And what makes you think he really wants to marry me? Particularly after I told him his leaving was for the best." With a shake of her head, Elizabeth bit off the head of the gingerbread man.

"*I* really don't believe she'd want to marry me, Thomas. Not after her parting words." Angus and Thomas sat on the deck of Martin and Christie's house. Jag lay in between, but with his paw on Thomas' foot.

"I really believe she does. Disagreements happen, harsh words get spoken, and you really weren't clear about your motivation for leaving. Can't blame her for misunderstanding."

"Well, I don't. Nor do I know how to remedy things. I'm respecting her privacy."

"Which isn't going to get you back together, is it? At least you'll have to see her at Christmas dinner."

"About that. Perhaps I should spend the evening with George."

"He's going to Sylvia's. You're not getting out of it that easy. Besides, I'm back in the bride's good books so don't make me have to break it to her you don't like her cooking." His expression was so serious it made Angus laugh, and Thomas joined in.

Jag sat up at the laughter and offered his paw to Thomas. "You're a fine dog, Jag. Will you keep him, Angus?"

"Might not be an option." Trev climbed the steps, a dog lead in one hand. "Afternoon, gentlemen."

"What do you mean?" Thomas put his hand on Jag's head. "He's perfectly fine here."

Trev leaned against the railing. "So I see. Seems his owner had a living relative after all. A nephew in the city."

"Not a city dog."

"He's taken a real shine to you, Thomas. Look, probably won't amount to anything, but the ranger is heading over now to collect him, check for a microchip and other identification."

"So, tell them to come here. Don't they have some fancy portable machine for microchips?"

"They do, but he's got to go back with her. Due process and all that. Sorry."

Thomas looked away, out to the horizon, hand still on Jag's head.

Trev squatted near Jag. "Hey, doggie. Let's put this on." He reached for the dog's collar, but Jag backed away.

"Jag, sit." Thomas held his hand out for the lead. "Be a good dog."

He clipped the lead onto the collar and handed the end to Trev. "You find a way to bring him back. Angus needs him."

Angus and Trev exchanged a glance, then Trev stood again. "I'm sorry, mate. I'll let you know."

"Thanks, Trev, we know you will." Angus patted Thomas' shoulder as Trev and Jag went down the steps.

Eyes back on the horizon, Thomas blinked a few times. "See, Angus. You love them and they leave. Don't lose Elizabeth."

"*D*o we have final numbers yet, or should I ring around to be certain?" Christie and Martin were in the salon after hours, using the spa. The salon itself was in darkness, except for a lamp on the reception counter. Out here under a clear roof, they could see the stars above. The bubbles were off, only low jets circulating the water and providing some relief for Christie's sore back.

Martin reached for their wine glasses and handed one to Christie. "Everyone is invited, and I'm not stressed about whether they turn up or not. Any spare food will be put to good use on Christmas morning."

"The shelter in Green Bay?"

"Small as that town might be, there are too many people struggling and we're not."

Christie leaned closer and kissed Martin. "Yet another reason I love you. Do you always do this?"

"Most years. Thomas took me along every Christmas Day for as long as I can recall. Even when we had little. Always said generosity is its own reward."

Randall padded over from where he'd been asleep in the middle of the new garden. Grass now replaced the original concrete yard and herbs and roses grew in front of a hedge of fast growing narrow pines, planted as semi-mature trees to ensure privacy for the clients.

As Randall flopped down on the deck around the spa, Christie reached out to scratch behind his ear. "I'm so sad for Thomas. Hopefully Jag will come back and he'll be able to see him again."

"Dogs love the man. He really needs his own one again, but he's not prepared to take a puppy on. Knows his limitations."

Christie sank back into the spa, wiggling around until she found the perfect spot. This week, before Christmas was almost over and much as she loved her new business, exhaustion almost overwhelmed her.

"Sweetheart, on Sunday I want you to take it easy. Tomorrow you'll be working all day again and I can see how tired you are." Martin glanced up at the sky. "This was a good idea."

"It was your idea." Christie smiled and sipped her wine. "So, back to Christmas Eve. Who do we know is coming along? Thomas and Martha of course, and Angus."

"Daphne and John. Aunt Sylvia and the brat. And Jess."

Christie giggled. "The 'brat', as you call Belinda, is my right hand here."

"And I love her to bits. Barry. Trev, as long as nothing crops up like it normally does when we celebrate anything. Elizabeth."

"Is she? I mean, has she told you she'll be there for certain?"

"Is this why you asked about ringing around earlier? I hope she will be there. And I hope she and Angus sort this out, but it isn't our job to do it for them. Is it?" He brushed a stray hair from Christie's eyes, smiling at her expression. "Finish the wine and I'll get you home. Let you have some sleep."

21

NO SHAME OR BLAME

"*D*o you think if I put a bow on you with a card from Martin to Granddad, he might get the hint?" Thomas and Randall ambled down the cottage driveway as the Lotus, with Christie and Martin inside, drove away. "Be the best Christmas present ever, eh?"

Randall wagged his tail, eyes on Thomas, until he heard the back door open. Thomas watched the dog disappear around the corner of the cottage.

At least you're here today.

The morning was already hot, with temperatures forecast to soar later in the day.

"There you are. I've made some lemonade if you'd like a glass?" Martha was on the back porch with Randall, who barely glanced up from the bowl of water he lapped from.

"Take a whole jug if I stay out here too long." Thomas followed Martha inside and a moment later Randall padded through the back door. "Still haven't got the hang of closing doors, have you, dog?"

Martha poured lemonade into two tall glasses already half filled with ice. "Is he here for the day?"

"Hope so. Youngsters are going to Warrnambool. Some kind of farmers market on so Martin thought he'd have a look for the party tomorrow night. Apparently Christie is behind with her Christmas shopping, so she refused Martin's suggestion of breakfast in bed."

Randall went into the dining room where he loved the cool of the timber floor beneath the table, so Martha and Thomas made their way there. The trunk still occupied the sideboard.

"Better move it out and make space for Christmas dinner." Thomas nodded at it. "I'll put it back in the entry if you like."

"What do you think happened to all of Dorothy's dolls? There's nothing in her diary about them, but they must have been valuable, going all the way back to the mid-1800s."

"Not in her estate?"

"Angus never mentioned them. Nor did Christie."

"You'd think she'd have kept them for her own children."

Martha almost snorted. "The daughter she alienated? Or the grandchild she treated like a stranger? From the time she moved to Melbourne, she lost any interest in being generous, or compassionate, or kind, or—"

Thomas put a hand over hers. "The complete opposite of her little sister. Who is all of those things and so much more."

As if expelling her irritation with Dorothy, Martha drew in a long breath, and exhaled slowly.

"Better?"

"I think I'm going to be on edge until I know... well, it isn't my business, as I said on the jetty, but..."

"But you'd like to open the shoebox?"

"Unless you've changed your mind."

"It needs opening. There might be nothing in there to answer any questions. Or something to make the situation worse. With George, I mean, because we're good now. Aren't we?" He squeezed Martha's hand and she curled up the corners of her mouth with a nod.

"I'll ring George. See if he's up to visitors."

1 *993*

Not content to give George the trunk and keys to the cottage, Dorothy Ryan drove there ahead of him. He wondered how she fitted her new red Range Rover through the laneways of Melbourne. Such a big vehicle for city use. He stopped worrying about her transport problems as they turned onto the road to the old cottage.

Once the home of his best friend, he'd not been here since the day Thomas left, after helping him pack the last of his belongings. His parents had gone, he was about to marry Frances, and the cottage only held bad memories.

How the place had deteriorated. Overgrown bushes, the weatherboard walls peeling, the driveway pitted with holes from years with no maintenance. George parked on the opposite side of the road as Dorothy drove through the open gate. By the time she was at the back of the Range Rover, he'd crossed the road.

"Hurry up, George. I don't want anyone seeing us here."

"Nobody ever comes up here now." Nevertheless, he reached for the trunk.

"Wait." Dorothy pushed between George and the trunk. She inserted a key into the lock and opened the lid just enough to peek inside. George couldn't see past her and wasn't interested in what she kept in there. A click and she'd locked it again, taking the key and burying into a pocket. "Pick it up and follow me."

He regretted agreeing to this. But the alternative was to face public and possibly police accusations and a probe into the actions of his family. And him. His jewellery shop was his life.

At the back door, Dorothy fussed as she found the right key, then pushed the door open and instructed George to go ahead. She closed and locked the door before stomping down the hallway in her expensive leather high-heeled boots. It crossed George's mind that she had done very well for herself with the business degree her mother forced her to do.

"Once you get this up there, make it invisible. Push it right under an eave and then come straight down again. And remember. Tell nobody. Ever!"

He'd nodded, unable to find words. How he missed Martha, such the opposite of this aggressive, rude woman. But Martha was long gone, and now Thomas was once again alone, apart from his little grandson.

"You look so deep in thought, George." Martha put a cup of herbal tea in front of him at his kitchen table. "Are you feeling alright, dear?"

Must everyone keep asking this?

"Quite well, thank you. I was thinking about my godson."

"He didn't leave your side for hours, George. When you were unconscious, he watched over you." Thomas sat opposite, placing a shoebox on the table. "Martin loves you deeply. As do I."

"I regret worrying you all. And I'm feeling better than I have in months."

"So you'll keep taking the medication and cut back on the hours at the shop?"

"Not sure about the shop, Thomas. But yes, I want to see my godson's children, so I've taken this as a wakeup call." George pointed to his tea. "See, even off the caffeine and regrettably, the whiskey. For now."

Underneath the table, Randall sighed and rolled over to sleep, touching George's foot. "So why do you have Randall?"

"The children are Christmas shopping. Too hot to leave him at home, besides, he needs time with Martha."

"I see." George smiled. "And this?" He nodded at the shoebox. Something about it was familiar.

"The reason we're here when Martin is not in town." Thomas glanced at Martha as she joined them. "But I need to know you're up to a bit of history. Maybe something good, perhaps not. Don't want to be calling an ambulance."

The shoebox was old and faded. "I remember these boxes. And the ribbon." The past wasn't going away. When he'd first had some coherent thoughts in hospital, it was of his conversation with Martha. None of it mattered now. The secrets were out and Thomas was still his best friend. "Why was Martin with me in the hospital, Thomas? Not you?"

"I was getting this from the cabin." Thomas undid the ribbon, letting the velvet strip coil on the table.

"You're not making much sense."

"Apparently you asked for someone, dear. Before you really woke up." Martha's eyes flicked between his and the shoebox. "You wanted to see Frannie."

Shame poured into George and he dropped his head.

How could this be?

Bad enough they knew he'd helped Dorothy hide the trunk, but now... how would Thomas forgive him?

"You can stop it right now. George, nothing's changed. You never did anything wrong, and if anything, I'm the one who took Frances from you."

"No, Tom, George. Frannie was always in love with you, Thomas. We never saw it. And George, with Thomas single she wouldn't give up until she married him. If anyone is to blame, it is me for leaving."

George shook his head. "Perhaps we all need to stop blaming ourselves and move forward."

"Exactly my point of getting this from the cabin." Thomas took the lid off. "Frannie kept it with her precious bits and pieces and I never opened it, not even after she died."

"Do you remember she worked at the fabric shop for a long time? The shoebox is from there. Had several pairs I bought over the years."

"Oh, George, what a good memory you have! I quite forgot they sold shoes as well as fabric and ribbon." Martha picked up the velvet. "So, two boxes with red ribbon. One with Tom's letters to me and the rings."

"And whatever is in here." Thomas moved the box so it was between them all. "Shall we?"

22

MISGUIDED LOVE

*M*artha's heart raced as Thomas reached into the shoebox. She wished Christie was here, yet knew it was for the best that this moment was shared by the two men who'd mattered to Frannie. Shared with her, Frannie's best friend for so long. Her fingers curled into her palms.

One by one, Thomas laid out the contents of the box.

A thick, sealed envelope.

A small notebook.

A black velvet jewellery pouch.

George gasped.

"George? Isn't this one of yours?" Thomas asked.

With a nod, George gently opened and emptied the contents onto his palm. Out slid a silver chain. His hands visibly shook as he lifted the chain to reveal a pendant. A silver letter 'F'.

"Oh! You made this for Frannie, George." Martha leaned closer to inspect the pendant. "She kept it all those years."

"But… but she told me she'd lost it." George's eyes glinted. "I don't understand."

Thomas sighed, and took one of Martha's hands. "I found it. In the cottage. From… that night."

That night.

After Frannie took off her clothes in a failed seduction attempt.

"I see." She gripped Thomas' hand. "You kept it?"

"Not on purpose. I did find it the night you left me, but Frannie was the last person I wanted to see for a while. It went into a drawer and it was only when I moved out of the cottage it reappeared."

"Well, I'm glad you have it back, George." Martha released Thomas' hand and picked up the pouch. "There's something in here. A note." She smoothed the paper out, revealing Frannie's handwriting. "Keepsake from George Campbell. A sweet and dear man."

"I'm touched." George nodded to himself with a small smile. He returned the pendant to the pouch, then studied the note before refolding and putting it into his top pocket.

"Notebook, or envelope?" Thomas had one hand on each.

"Do you think we should do this?" All of a sudden, doubt flooded into Martha. What if there were personal memories of Frannie's intimate life with Thomas? Or more about her conspiracy with Dorothy? She knew now how the trunk got to the cottage, but still not why the other shoebox, the one containing her wedding and engagement rings and all the letters Thomas wrote trying to win her back, was inside it.

"Up to you, bride. Last thing I want is to upset you, or you." Thomas looked at George. "There's a reason Frannie kept these things though, and if it gives you both, and me, some peace of mind, then I vote we do."

With a touch of his top pocket, George nodded. They both turned to Martha.

"Very well. But then it's done. We put it all behind us."

Thomas picked up the envelope. "No stamp." He turned it over. "No names, nothing. Let's take a look inside." He grinned suddenly. "Could be money."

Martha rolled her eyes. "Open it, old man. Surprised you didn't suggest it had a restaurant voucher inside."

"There's a thought." He broke the seal and lifted the flap. "Err... you two won't believe this." Thomas pulled out a letter, and a wad of twenty dollar notes. Crisp, perfectly lined up and tied with string. "I was joking."

"They look brand new."

"They are, I think." Thomas peered at the top note. "Feel new, but look how old they are. Must be from the sixties, maybe seventies." He counted the wad and his jaw dropped. "There's one thousand dollars here."

"May I?" Martha slid the letter closer. "This is Dorothy's handwriting. I wonder if this is the final key to the past."

1971

Dorothy Ryan counted the notes again. Surely one thousand dollars would secure the silence of the only person who could harm her reputation. And reputation meant everything to a young woman in a business world filled with male contenders ready to pounce on her hard-won career. One day, this amount of money would be there in her bank account for the taking, but the notes she now tied with string were a secret gift from her mother.

Lilian owed her this. It was her mother who'd refused to accept Thomas Blake as a suitable suitor for Martha. Lilian who'd turned her back on her youngest daughter's engagement party, leaving Dorothy to make decisions which led to such disastrous consequences. With a heavy sigh, Dorothy slipped the cash into an envelope.

Martha was gone, travelling somewhere overseas with no contact for the past two years or more. Father heard from her from time to time, but not one word to her sister, as if she somehow suspected the truth. Regret stabbed Dorothy and she put down the unsealed envelope, and gazed at her favourite photograph. How different things might have been. But they weren't. It was important the secrets she shared with Frances Blake stayed secret. Dorothy took a pad of fine writing paper from a drawer.

Dear Frances,

Once you read this, destroy the letter. This serves as our final communication.

You will find a sum of money enclosed. Use it however you wish, but understand this is in exchange for your silence, now and in the future. No good will come of bringing our past association to the notice of your husband, my sister, or any other person. I am confident you would not wish your son to know your part in the fallout from our regrettable relationship.

For I do regret what happened to my sister, more than she will ever know. You may have what you wanted – the husband and son rightfully belonging to Martha – but I have nothing from this.

My sister is lost to me. All that remains are the memories of our childhood. The dolls we'd play with. The songs I would sing to Martha, hoping one day to perform to a wider audience. Regrets follow me everywhere. The photograph that accompanies this note is a reminder to you of what you helped destroy. Remember this before you divulge a word.

Dorothy Lilian Ryan

"*M*artha? Look... this was inside the envelope." Thomas held an old photograph.

She didn't want to see it. Turmoil bubbled through her veins, into her heart. Such cruel words to Frannie. To use her own son against her. Yet the bitterness about Dorothy's own destiny cut her deeply. Mother forbade Dorothy to follow her dreams and directed her into the commercial world, expecting she'd come home to River's End and revive their flagging timber business.

Instead, Dorothy accepted a lucrative job in the city. And when the timber yards closed, their parents boarded up Palmerston House and moved to Ireland. She was left with no family or friends.

Martha folded the letter and put it down, then finally looked at the photograph. Two girls. Five-year-old Martha sat on fourteen-year-old Dorothy's lap, playing with one of the precious dolls from the trunk. Both were laughing. A happy moment captured forever. *The photo-*

graph that accompanies this note is a reminder to you of what you helped destroy.

Thomas stood and came around behind Martha, putting his hands on her shoulders. "She loved you."

"And I... loved her." Martha put her head in her hands and wept.

23

FIRST CHRISTMAS EVE

*M*artin pushed the gate to his property wide open, and latched it onto the fence. The afternoon was cooler than the last few days and he was almost finished preparing for the party tonight.

Christmas Eve.

First one married. He smiled to himself.

"What's that cheesy grin for, son?" Thomas, followed closely by Randall, carried two tall garden candles from the house.

"Christie." Martin took one of the candles from Thomas and pushed the sharp end of its stick deep into the ground inside the gate. "Our first Christmas."

"Here, you're stronger than me." Thomas handed Martin the second candle. "Know what you mean. Our first Christmas as well. As husband and wife."

"And we will celebrate both events tonight."

"And tomorrow."

Job done, the men wandered toward the house. Randall trotted ahead, found a long patch of grass, and began to roll. Between the long, jasmine covered railing of the deck, and the edge of the cliff, a marquee was set up with a couple of long trestle tables and chairs.

Thomas had strung solar lights and tinsel around it, as well as the deck.

"Looks inviting, Thomas. Thanks for the help." Martin led the way up the steps and through to the kitchen. "Drink?"

"Water's good for now."

"When are you heading back for Martha?"

"Soon, unless you need more help."

"Not much to do until later on. Is she okay?"

Thomas sat at the counter and Martin leaned against the opposite side, both with glasses of water. "Bit rattled. Last thing we expected was a letter from the past. We're going to leave the notebook be for the moment."

"And the money?"

Thomas shrugged.

Randall wandered in, tail plumed high. He plonked himself beside Thomas and rolled onto his side. "Good idea to have a nap, dog. Once guests arrive, you'll be run off your feet."

"What about me?" Martin finished his water.

"It was your idea, so no sympathy here. When will Angus get back?"

"Not his keeper, Thomas."

"I just wanted some friendlier company." Thomas grinned and stood. "I'll go find the bride." He grabbed a box of tinsel on his way out.

Martin started on the platters. One at a time he piled them high with seafood salad, a fresh garden salad, his own twist on potato salad, and a fruit platter. Each went into the fridge once done. Then, he worked on a cheese board.

Angus arrived as Martin was cleaning down the counter. With a smile, he put a box onto the coffee table. A big box, filled with little gift wrapped boxes. "The craft shop was wonderful! I can't believe they did all of this so quickly."

Martin joined him and picked one of the small boxes up. "The size is perfect. This is going to be fun."

"Where shall I put them? All under the tree, or piled on one of the tables?"

"We might let Christie decide. She's feeling a bit left out today, but should be here soon."

"In that case, I might go and change."

"Angus, thanks for picking them up. Between you and Thomas, it's made my job much easier today."

"A pleasure. I'll be right back to help set things out." His phone rang and he pulled it from a pocket. "Oh, it's Trev. Back shortly."

Martin gazed after Angus. He seemed happier today. Perhaps looking forward to tonight. Or seeing Elizabeth.

"*B*ut, doll, don't you think it should wait until after Christmas Day? We still have to get ready for the party, and goodness, look at the time!" Daphne threw her phone into her handbag. "We should close now."

With a laugh, John headed for the front door. "Very well. An hour early won't upset anyone. Not on Christmas Eve." He locked the door and turned the sign.

"Thank you. But about the display—"

"It won't take me long to set it up. Elizabeth insisted it be done as soon as the board arrived. Which, as you can see, is now here."

Daphne pouted as she glared at the oversized timber board leaning against the window, along with a long spike and John's tools. It was a pretty sign in spite of her irritation, with the main photo showing off the foyer of Palmerston House, then a smaller photo of the pond area, and another of the kitchen.

"Well, I'm going to need a while to get ready so are you doing this now, or on the way to the party?"

John came back around the counter and held his arms out. Daphne stopped pouting and went into his embrace. "Daph, you go home and take as much time as you need, but you always look wonderful. I'll drop around to Palmerston and get this set up, then I'm done until after Boxing Day."

"Promise?" Daphne's voice was muffled against his chest. "We'll have some time together?"

"We work together every day, love. But I get what you mean." He released her and reached for his own phone from behind the counter. "How about we have a serious talk after Christmas? It might be time to plan for the caravan you want and a bit of travel."

"Oh, love!" Daphne threw her arms around John. "Yes, let's do exactly that!" She planted a kiss on his lips.

"Well, if this is the response to the idea, we do need to talk." John kissed her back. "Go get ready. I'll be there soon."

A few moments later, as she let herself out of the back door, it occurred to Daphne she'd never found out why John was so secretive about Angus visiting that time. And now with Palmerston House on the market, what would happen to dear Elizabeth and Angus? Nothing had been said about finding them a home of their own, so what was going on?

---

*C*hristmas music, laughter, conversation. Christie heard the wonderful sounds from the gate, where she and Randall had gone to look out for Thomas and Martha. Even though it wasn't quite dark, all the solar lights looked lovely, and someone – she suspected Thomas – had added tinsel to the gate. She couldn't remember seeing it open like this before. Nor, it seemed, had anyone else, as all the cars were parked along the street.

Arriving home only a couple of hours ago, she'd been amazed at their transformed house. The marquee, a second Christmas tree on the deck, a dance floor set up outside. How Martin had done this, and prepared all the cold food, was beyond her. All she'd had to do was decide where their gifts to the guests should be, accept a glass of wine, and take a shower. Even Angus had smiled more than she'd seen in days.

"Ah, there you are."

"I was just thinking about you, Angus." Christie kissed his cheek as he stopped beside her. "Thanks for helping Martin today."

"The least I can do, seeing as you are both being so generous about my staying here."

"You're most welcome, although I do hope..."

"So do I. She does appear to be running late."

"So are Martha and Thomas. They went to pick up George first."

"This looks like them." Angus nodded to the road.

The four wheel drive spluttered as Thomas reduced speed and turned through the gateway. His window was wound down and he stopped beside Christie and Angus. "Special delivery. Might go closer so George doesn't have to walk too far."

"We'll follow."

Thomas nosed toward the side of the house and, by the time Angus and Christie caught up, was opening the front passenger door. Randall danced about at Thomas' feet.

"Who put tinsel on your collar?" Martha opened the back door and climbed down, accepting Angus hand. "Thank you, dear."

Christie and Thomas helped George out, who leaned back against the door once it closed. He put a hand onto Angus' shoulder. "Terribly sorry, Angus."

"George?"

"It was a shock to us when we drove past, so I can only imagine how you feel."

"I'm not sure I follow." Angus cast a puzzled glance at Thomas.

"You don't know." Thomas said.

"Auntie, did these two start on the Christmas cheer early? They are not making much sense."

"No, but I think I'd like some now." Martha took Angus' hand. "When we drove past Palmerston House, there was a big sign out the front. Elizabeth appears to have put it up for sale."

"She's selling Palmerston House?" Christie shook her head. "Elizabeth would never do that!"

"If the board out the front is correct, then she is. Through John." George took his cane from Thomas.

Christie looked from George, to Thomas, then Martha. Elizabeth loved her home.

But maybe she loves Angus more.

"Angus—"

But he was already moving. Christie sprinted after him. "You're going to see her?" She caught him near the gate.

"I am."

"Shall I drive you?"

"The walk will do me good."

"Then, I'll come—"

"Miss Christie, you have guests. I shall return in due course." He didn't slow or turn his head. "I must do this alone."

In a moment he'd disappeared into the night.

24

AN EVEN PLAYING FIELD

*A*s she turned on the outside lights, Elizabeth softly hummed a love song she'd heard on the radio the first day she'd met Angus. For some reason it was stuck in her head. All day he'd been in her thoughts, even more than usual. Well, she would see him soon, at Christie and Martin's party, as long as he was there, of course.

When John arrived earlier to put up the board, she'd almost told him to take it away. It was real. Her beautiful, stately home for the past twenty plus years was going to be sold. After he left, she'd wandered the gardens, then sat in the front living room for a while. So many memories filled this place. From the early years here with Keith, her childhood sweetheart, to the year just gone.

She'd found her old friend Martha again. Met Martha's great-niece Christie under less happy circumstances, not imagining they would also become friends. Charlotte Dean had been a guest for most of the year, and she missed her, now Charlotte had moved to the Macedon Ranges. So many celebrations. Two weddings. Even some danger.

All in all, the years had been kind to Elizabeth, and to Palmerston House. It was the right time to do this. Angus made sense by moving out and it was only after much soul-searching she'd understood what motivated him.

The flashing lights on the Christmas tree reminded her to switch them off. They were wasted anyway, with only herself here. She turned them off, picked up her handbag and a paper carry bag filled with small presents, and went to the front door.

She glanced behind at the darkened foyer, with the tree a beautifully decorated sentinel. Decorated with Angus. Elizabeth smiled and opened the door.

Angus stood on the doorstep, his hand raised to knock.

---

*A*ll the way down the hill, Angus' thoughts had spun. Why would Elizabeth sell the home she'd cherished for so long? Was his leaving the reason she wanted to go? To leave River's End? Where would she live? Or did she no longer wish to run her business? Yet, she loved looking after her guests and making each one of them feel special.

He'd halted before going down the driveway, staring at the large board now dominating the fence line. In its history, Palmerston House was sold once, and that was to Elizabeth and Keith. Before then, it belonged to generation after generation of the Ryan family. Martha grew up here. Only one other person had owned the property, William Temple, who built the house.

The first time he'd been here, it was to stay for a short visit. Time to spend with Christie. But Elizabeth kept him here. Apart from a few weeks away to attend to business, he'd become a long-term guest, liking everything about the sprawling property and the woman who owned it.

Loving everything.

The outside light turned on, so he left the sign and strode along the driveway. With every step, his heart beat a little faster and his resolve got a little stronger. Elizabeth needed to explain this so he could understand. And she needed to come to the party, where her friends would help put a smile back on her lovely face.

On the verandah, he raised his hand to knock. The door swung open before he made contact, and there was Elizabeth. All dressed up and with a radiant smile.

Which dropped when she made eye contact. She hadn't known he was there.

How could she?

He pulled his shoulders back, ready with words of support and understanding, rehearsed on the way.

"Elizabeth, you cannot sell Palmerston House!"

Oh, my!

Those were not the words he'd expected to say. Elizabeth would tell him to leave. Shut the door in his face and who would blame her. He opened his mouth to apologise but nothing came out.

"Actually, I can." Elizabeth stepped aside. "Do you want to come in?"

Angus was in the foyer before she changed her mind. The Christmas tree's lights were off and the foyer in darkness.

"You look... so pretty."

"Oh!"

She blushed. Angus ignored the inner voice reciting all the reasons this was a mistake. He closed the door.

"Allow me to rephrase my first statement into a question. Why are you selling your home, dear lady?"

"Did you leave Palmerston House because you wanted us on an even playing field, for want of a better term? Angus, were you concerned because I own such an expensive property and you were a guest here, rather than having your own home?"

He nodded.

Elizabeth drew her breath in audibly. "By sell... selling Palmerston House, I'm giving us an even playing field."

The grandfather clock slowly chimed seven o'clock. Angus reached both his hands out. Without hesitation, Elizabeth put her own hands in his.

"My sweet Elizabeth. You humble me with your kindness. I have no answers, not yet, but your happiness means more to me than my own pride, so please, don't sell your home. Not for me."

"I'd sacrifice everything, Angus, anything, to have your love back," Elizabeth whispered.

Without letting go of her hands, Angus dropped to one knee. "You've always had my love. And this is probably the silliest time to ask, but will you marry me? Will you?"

25

SMALL MIRACLES

"*D*id you know Angus moved out?" Daphne, empty champagne glass in hand, trailed behind Christie toward the kitchen, away from the music and laughter outside.

"He's been staying here with us. Daph, don't take it personally. If he and Elizabeth wanted it common knowledge, they'd have said something."

"Common knowledge? But she's my friend!"

Christie put down an empty platter and hugged Daphne. "I didn't mean it like it sounded. Here, have some more champagne. You need to remember they never once called themselves a couple."

"So who does know? John is in so much trouble for keeping this to himself."

As she poured champagne into Daphne's glass, Christie smiled. "Poor John. He must have been in a difficult situation with Elizabeth insisting on secrecy about selling, and Angus the same about getting his own place. And as far as I know, the only other people who knew were Thomas and Martha, and only because Elizabeth mentioned it at the hospital when they asked about Angus."

Daphne gave an exaggerated sigh. "Well, perhaps it was for the best. I'd have wanted to help them through it. Offer some counselling when they might not be ready yet."

"You're very sweet." Christie picked up a tray of pastries. "And so is Sylvia for bringing all of these."

"What's sweet is the present from you and Martin." Daphne beamed and dug around in the oversized bag slung over her shoulder. "You are both so clever!" She pulled out a snow globe, turned it upside-down, and then watched as snowflakes fluttered over River's End beach. "We'll take this on our caravan trips."

"We wanted something to remind people of home, no matter where they are. And being Christmas, thought the snowflakes were perfect." Christie took another look. "Martin designed them."

"Well, everyone loves them. I'll bring the champagne bottle. And go and apologise to John. I do hope Angus and Elizabeth are talking things through."

"I can't help but blame myself for putting the idea into Angus' head." George sat beneath the marquee with Thomas and Martha as they finished off their plates. "It was an innocent comment, but set things in motion, I fear."

"There's little point in second guessing yourself, George. It may have happened anyway, so you should concentrate on your health." Martha refilled his glass of sparkling water.

"Would love some whiskey instead."

"We all want things we can't have, so stop complaining." Thomas cut a slice of cheese. "I'd like Randall to duplicate himself, for example."

"It is Christmas, dear."

"Time of miracles? Don't know if they extend so far."

Martha looked past Thomas toward the gate. "Speaking of miracles..."

Thomas and George followed her line of sight. Angus and Elizabeth emerged from the darkness, their hands entwined. At first, nobody else noticed, then one by one, each guest stopped talking and formed a semi-circle around the couple.

"Please, don't let us interrupt the festivities," Angus said.

Christie abruptly halted halfway down the steps. "Elizabeth? Angus?"

"Is John here?" Elizabeth asked, eyes sparkling.

"I am." John, with Daphne on his arm, stepped forward. "Is everything alright?"

Elizabeth glanced at Angus, then back at John. "We need to apologise for causing you such inconvenience. And I'll pay you for any costs, of course. But it appears I may not be selling Palmerston House after all."

A murmur passed through the group, then fell silent as Angus spoke.

"Certain decisions are still to be made, but I'm so very delighted to tell you all, our family, and friends that Elizabeth has agreed to marry me."

Daphne squealed, Christie jumped down the rest of the steps, Martha clapped, and George pushed himself to his feet. In seconds, Angus and Elizabeth were surrounded, being kissed and hugged, and having their hands shaken. Martin and Thomas opened more champagne and the whole party toasted the love and future of Angus and Elizabeth.

Much later, when most of the guests had gone home, Thomas and Martha again sat with George. Angus had packed his suitcases and escorted Elizabeth back to Palmerston House, sharing a snow globe. Inside, Christie and Martin finished the last of the cleaning. They'd insisted they needed no help, and Randall, exhausted, followed them in. Music and laughter was replaced by the endless ocean waves below the cliff.

Martha opened her handbag. "I believe there's something we need to attend to." She drew out the notebook from the shoebox. "After our small miracle tonight, I feel it is the right time to see what Frannie kept in here."

"Should we wait for the other two?" Thomas glanced at the open sliding door.

"Martin would not accept us reading his grandmother's notebook. It might not be a diary, but he'd see it as personal."

"Open it, Martha." George said.

The notebook was small and there was little writing inside. A couple of shopping lists, crossed off. A phone number with no name. Then, toward the middle, some dates with notes.

7 August 1971

Ten o'clock at Green Bay. Meet with D.R. Take shoebox with rings, photographs, and my diary.

"Diary?" Martha gave Thomas a questioning glance but he shrugged. She went past several more blank pages.

24 December 1971

Very last day at the fabric shop! Buy presents for my family at lunch break.

"I'd sold two paintings that month and landed a commission. All Frannie ever wanted was to stay home with Thomas junior, so I'd told her it was time. She'd worked part time since we married." Thomas said.

7 August 1972

A year since I gave the shoebox to Dorothy Ryan. I wish I hadn't. My diary had poems to Thomas junior in it. And all the things I'd wished I'd have said to Martha. I'm so sorry for hurting her and tricking her. It was wrong.

The words caught in Martha's throat and she put the notebook down to take a sip of water. Thomas leaned over and kissed her cheek.

"Should I finish reading, Martha?" George offered.

She shook her head and reopened the small book. There was one more entry, on the very last page.

Whatever is in the envelope will remain a mystery to me. Perhaps when Thomas junior is grown, I'll give it to him to help him on his way. But it is not mine. I have everything I need with my little family.

"Oh, Frannie never even opened it. She never read Dorothy's

letter." Martha closed the notebook and slid it into her handbag. "Tom, she knew she did the wrong thing."

Thomas stared out at the night sky, blinking a little too quickly. Martha took his hand and he squeezed it back. Tightly.

26

A WAY FORWARD

*C*hristie drove back from Green Bay, Martin at her side. Both were quiet, deep in their own thoughts. With plenty of fresh leftovers from the party packed into two eskies, they'd left after breakfast, Randall at home still asleep in his bed.

The shelter wasn't large, but today attracted a bigger than usual attendance of disadvantaged and homeless people. Older men, families, a few young adults all united by a need to find company on a day many of them would otherwise spend alone.

Martin was welcomed by the shelter workers like a long lost friend. Christie immediately got involved in preparing food. She talked to everyone, her smile infectious. As they went to leave, the coordinator patted Martin on the back and asked him to thank Thomas and Martha again.

"They must have been there so early." Christie slowed at the last few curves before River's End. "We couldn't have missed them by much."

"I'm pleased with their decision."

"About giving Frannie's money to the shelter?"

"Thomas didn't need to ask me though."

Last night, Thomas had filled Martin and Christie in on the

discovery of the money in the envelope, and the note that it might be used for Thomas junior.

"If my father never needed it, then it should go to those who do."

"I'm sure it will make a difference."

They passed the turn-off to the cottage and drove into the car park near the graveyard. The four wheel drive was parked there and Thomas and Martha reached it as Christie parked.

"Merry Christmas!" Thomas hugged Christie, then Martin. "Been to the shelter?"

"It was wonderful!" Christie put an arm around Martha. "But so sad. I'm thinking I'd like to do a bit more."

"Well, you made a great impression. You should have seen her. Piling up plates for serving, making sure anyone with special needs was put first, bringing a smile to everyone's face. I'm proud of you, sweetheart." Martin glanced at the graveyard. "Been visiting Mum and Dad?" he asked Thomas.

"Yup. Is that where you're heading?"

Christie reached into the back of the Lotus. "We've got some pretty bouquets." She handed two to Martin, and took two more out.

"Come on, old man." Martha reached for Thomas' hand. "Lots of preparation to do for tonight."

"We do. See you both tonight. Remember to bring my dog."

Once they'd driven out of the car park, Martin led the way to Dorothy's grave. "And I'm proud of you for this."

"What I've learnt about Gran from Martha recently gives me a little more insight into why she was the way she was. Pushed into a career she didn't want, forbidden to pursue her dreams, left to parent when her mother failed to." Christie laid one of the bouquets on the grave. "She was wrong in what she did to Martha. And my mother. But I did love her and now, I forgive her."

Martin held out a hand and she took it. He kissed her forehead. "Forgiveness is a way forward."

A little further away, Martin's family were laid side by side. His father, mother, and grandmother Frannie, all taken by a drunk driver on the same day. Every Christmas, Thomas would bring flowers to each grave. Until last year, when he'd discovered Frannie's part in destroying his relationship with Martha. Since then he'd boycotted Frannie's grave, not even tending the purple lobelia Martin planted.

"Look." Christie put her hand on Martin's arm. "There's flowers."

"Thomas was just here, sweetheart."

"No, look at Frannie's grave."

Surprise filled Martin's face and he knelt near the headstone. He gently placed a bouquet beside a beautiful wreath. "Granddad?"

Christie knelt at his side and slipped her arm around him. "Forgiveness is more than a way forward. It's a key to the door between the past and present."

27

THE CHRISTMAS KEY

*B*y the middle of the afternoon, the stationmaster's cottage was overflowing with delectable Christmas smells. Once Thomas finished setting the dining room table, he joined Martha in the kitchen.

"Not sure I can wait until dinner, bride." He sniffed the air. "How do you make it look so easy?"

Martha struck a pose, a tea towel in one hand and a basting spoon in the other.

"Told you at the children's wedding, you should have been a model."

"Actually, when I lived briefly in California, I did some modelling."

"You did what? Since when did you live—"

"Still have some surprises. Now, would you see if there is one more lettuce in the garden? Models need to watch their figures."

Thomas didn't know if she was serious until she opened the back door. "Along the path, through the gate." He grinned as he stepped onto the back porch.

There were plenty of lettuce there, so he took his time selecting the best one, then added a handful of basil. Never could have enough. Tonight was going to be the best Christmas dinner ever. Glorious food. Handing out presents. Playing with Randall. Planning yet another River's End wedding. Almost perfect.

As he reached the back porch, Trev came around the corner. In jeans and a T-shirt declaring 'Santa's helper', he carried a gift wrapped box. "Ah, just the man I want to see. Merry Christmas."

"Trev. Thanks. What is it?"

"Open it, dear." Martha opened the back door. "Here, I'll take those. Hello, Trev."

His hands free of lettuce and basil, Thomas accepted the box. "Coming inside?"

Martha hurried into the cottage and re-emerged almost immediately.

"Nope. On my way to see Mum for a late Christmas dinner. Open it."

Inside the box was a dog bowl.

"Nice. Thanks, I think, Randall might like a new one."

"He doesn't get the hint, eh Martha?" Trev disappeared down the driveway.

"What hint? Where are you going?" Thomas gave Martha a puzzled look, made even more so by the wide smile on her face. She stepped off the porch and took his hand.

"Come on."

Trev's car was parked across the driveway and he stood beside the passenger door. Once Thomas was halfway down the driveway, he reached for the handle. "Oh, and this is the other half of your present."

With a quick motion, Trev opened the door. A black flash tore out of the car and barrelled along the driveway, almost knocking into Thomas, who lifted Jag into his arms. Jag licked his face until he laughed, but when he gently returned the dog to the ground, Thomas' face was wet with tears.

Jag trotted over to say hello to Martha and she patted the top of his head.

"How? I mean, what does this mean?" Thomas looked from Martha to Trev.

"He's officially available for a new home. Kind of jumped the gun, so to speak, and gave the nephew a call myself. He lives in an apartment and when I mentioned I might know a suitable home, was very grateful."

"A suitable home." Thomas crossed the distance to Martha. "Us?"

Martha reached her hand to his face, brushing away the tears. "Yes, Tom. Us. I think he likes you very much."

"And I like you very much." Thomas kissed the tip of her nose. "Thank you."

"So, he's staying, or does he come to Mum's with me?"

Thomas pulled Trev in for a bear hug. "I'll never forget this. Safe travels."

Jag sat beside Martha, tail wagging. He whined as Trev left, but once he'd driven away, ran to Thomas again.

"My dog?"

"I think so, dear. Why don't you get him a drink and we'll show him around."

The Christmas table was ready. Delectable food, wine in crystal glasses, beautiful flowers, and one of Christie's brand new candles. Martin's gift had almost made her cry, but tonight was about joy, not tears. A box of handmade soy candles called *Jasmine Sea*. The scent was perfect and now she'd decided to start a line of candles to sell in the beauty salon.

She gazed at the people sharing this wonderful night with her. Martin, the love of her life, and a happy man with the new surfboard she'd sprung on him this morning. Great-aunt Martha, whose smile hadn't left her face since they arrived. Thomas. She never seen him so content and although Jag was responsible for much of it, she suspected his visit to Frannie's grave also laid some old sorrows to rest.

Dear Angus could barely take his eyes off Elizabeth, and they rarely stopped holding hands. The 'For Sale' board was already gone, and with another wedding in the air, the town was joking about what mystery from the past might emerge this time.

No more mysteries.

This little town was due for a long and happy time of peaceful living.

Randall nudged her leg under the table and she reached down to stroke his silky ears. All of a sudden another nose nudged her other leg and she grinned. No more debating over who owned Randall, as Jag was now declared another shared member of the family.

And this is the key to it all.

Working together, supporting one another, and always putting love above any differences. This was her family, all of them, and this cottage was home to anyone who needed it.

"Sweetheart?" Martin lifted his glass and everyone followed. "Would you like to make the first toast?"

Christie raised her glass, eyes glistening as she overflowed with happiness. "Merry Christmas."

A NOTE ABOUT RIVER'S END

The Town of Love

The dear residents of this fictional seaside town have been part of my life for more than fifteen years. I love them so much, no matter what their role is or how much they've appeared in the stories.

The Christmas Key winds up the series, yet I believe I'll return here again. If you enjoyed visiting this special world, please let me know with an email, or via social media.

One character who forced herself into the limelight was Charlotte Dean. I wasn't sure why she arrived in River's End during *Jasmine Sea*, but she insisted I write more about her in *The Secrets of Palmerston House*. She then convinced me she needs her own series.

Keep a look out for *The Charlotte Dean Mysteries*, or stay up to date by joining my email newsletter or following me on social media or Bookbub. I promise you will see some of your favourite River's End characters in her stories.

Thank you for joining me on this marvellous adventure. To the golden beach, the jetty, the stationmaster's cottage, Palmerston House, Martin's house on the cliff, Thomas' cabin in the mountains, all the shops and homes in town. For being there for the highs and lows, for danger, special moments, and a journey through time.

Randall and Jag say a special woof goodbye... or is it, see you later! From my heart to yours.

Phillipa

ABOUT THE AUTHOR

Phillipa lives just outside a beautiful town in country Victoria, Australia. She also lives in the many worlds of her imagination and stockpiles stories beside her laptop.

Apart from her family, Phillipa's great loves include music, reading, growing veggies, and animals of all kinds.

She loves hearing from readers and sends out a monthly email with news, competitions, author recommendations, and lots of other goodies.

www.phillipaclark.com

CPSIA information can be obtained
at www.ICGtesting.com
Printed in the USA
BVHW071056290121
599084BV00006B/114